HEARTLESS

A Richard Rogan Novel

KEITH ALLEN

Heartless (A Richard Rogan Novel)
InnerNinja Media
ISBN: 978-0615848006
First Edition, 2013

Dedication

For my wife,
who makes me
want to be a better man

1.

He lit a cigarette and sat on the corner of the musty mattress. The place smelled of guilt and shame. He looked over at the girl lying, legs wide open, against the headboard. She was so young. She would have had her whole life ahead of her.

"A surgeon," he said.

"Really? I bet you saw some crazy stuff," she said.

"Yes, dear, more than a fair share of misfortunes wound up on my table."

"What is it like? Saving lives and all that?"

He smiled. He liked when they were interested. It made it better. Like they cared about him. He took a long drag on his smoke and looked around at the antique white paint peeling off the walls. This used to be a nice hotel. Back when he was younger, this was the kind of place you would want to take a woman. Though back then, you had to rent the room for the whole night, and the hotel employed a cleaning staff.

"It used to be amazing. We were gods. Saving lives, helping people. No one questioned us either. Now, people question their doctors more than they question their hair dresser. Didn't used to be like that. Used to be we would tell you to take something and call us in the morning, and you damn well went home, took the pill, and called us in the morning."

He stared at her breasts while he talked, small little apples growing on a pretty little tree. *It's a real shame that the only person who is going to see them after tonight is the coroner*, he thought. She wore a simple white t-shirt and a pair of ripped jean shorts. Her blonde locks fell in unkempt tangles around her boney shoulders.

"At some point, it all went wrong. It was like one day I went home a doctor, drinking brandy in my office with new fathers and smoking a Marlboro in surgery, and the next I was a factory worker. Churning out surgeries for insurance dollars. All these rules, no more smoking in the surgery suite, no more smoking in the hospital, then no smoking anywhere on the grounds. Had to walk a block down and smoke at the newspaper stand."

"Why didn't you just quit?"

"Because I like to smoke, helps me think."

"No, why don't you quit being a doctor, silly."

He wondered that every day. Why keep pressing on? He had plenty of money, but some sort of delusion made him feel he was serving a higher good, that each time he sliced a patient open with his favorite scalpel he was doing the world a solid. After a tough surgery where he was tested and prevailed, he often told himself that if he would not have put in the effort, the long hours, and dealt with the debilitating stress, he may have let the future President of our fine country die on his table.

"I have more good to do."

"Your soldier about ready, doctor?" she asked, smirking. "You only paid for an hour."

"You know when it went wrong?" he asked, avoiding the question.

"No."

"Male nurses."

"Male nurses?"

"Yep, soon as boys came in and put on a pair of pastel scrubs instead of a white coat, the place started going to shit."

"I don't think I've had a male nurse."

"Used to be you'd slap a nurse on the ass if she did a good job. She'd giggle and go about her day. Now...now if you even think about thinking about slapping or pinching or touching a nurse's hind end you get charged with sexual harassment. In my mind, that switch happened when men started being nurses."

The *squeak, squeak, squeak* of a customer getting satisfied could be heard overhead. The surgeon looked up and watched as tiny granules of ancient plaster drifted down from the ceiling above. It was almost time now. He used to hate this part, but now it was the part he looked forward to the most. The others had been practice; this was game time, the real deal. He had to do everything by the book.

"What did you give me? It's making me sleepy," she asked.

She rubbed her track-marked arms and pulled her knees into her chest. "I don't feel so good," she said as her eyes began to blink. Her head bobbed to her knees. "What did you give me?"

"Just something for the pain, dear," said the surgeon, sliding on a pair of latex gloves.

"What, what are you doing? I thought we were going to have some fun."

"Oh we are. I know I'm getting older, honey, but I'm still one of the best around." The scalpel in his hand reflected the thin trails of light from the neon sign outside the window.

Her doe brown eyes got big one last time as she stared at the blade. Then her forehead plunged to her knees. She was still—a limp ball of bones covered by flesh. The surgeon stood up from the end of the bed and walked over to where she lay.

"Sleep now, angel. I know you may not understand now, but when you look down from above, you'll see that this had to be done. You are a part of something bigger. Someone's life is at stake. Someone important."

✳ ✳ ✳

He ran as if he had seen a ghost—because he had. Normal people would respond with fear followed by a rapid retreat. Instead, Richard Rogan chased *after* the ghost. Rogan, who preferred no one know that he possessed a first name, chased the apparition down the hallway of the decaying hotel, feet pounding on the gold, diamond-patterned carpet. The mist moved with purpose, almost with poise, as it rounded the corner.

Rogan whipped around the bend with less finesse than the misty ghost. His red Converse shoes slipped on the aging patina, and he slid shoes-first, like a baseball player stealing second, right into a marble table, knocking the dusty flower arrangement to the floor. Rogan got to his feet just as the mist disappeared through the stairwell door. He ran to the door and carefully placed his hands against the steel. The door was cold against his palms, a good sign. He quickly popped the swinging door inward and heard a yelp from the other side. A female voice. He had never heard an apparition speak before.

"What the hell, Rogan?"

"Mac?"

"Yeah, you dolt. Thanks for slamming the door in my face. I swear to god if you broke my glasses again…"

Mac, known to everyone else in her life as McKenzie, glared at Rogan through her crooked, dark-rimmed glasses. She was slender, with fiery red hair, an outward sign of her inward personality.

"Did you see…anything?" asked Rogan.

"Got a real awesome look at the back of a door. Other than that, just you sprinting out of the room like your ass was on fire."

"But nothing in the stairway?"

"No, nothing. What are you talking about, Rogan? And why did you freak up there? We were having a really good EVP session."

EVPs, or Electronic Voice Phenomena, were unexplainable recorded sounds that resembled voices. Ghost hunters, Rogan and McKenzie included, capture these sounds at known haunted locations using high fidelity voice recorders. A session consisted of sitting in the dark and asking questions to the spirit that inhabited the location.

"I know, but I saw...something," said Rogan.

"Something? Care to elaborate, considering you streaked out and ran down two floors?"

"I think it was a full body apparition, but it was misty. I couldn't see details."

"Are you freakin' kidding me? That is awesome, what did it look like?" asked McKenzie.

"It looked like mist. Where's Troll and Angus?"

"They're down in 616 setting up for the next spot. Going all in down there," said McKenzie, fiddling with her glasses.

"Did I break 'em?"

"No, just twisted," said McKenzie with a sigh. "Let's go down to 6, maybe your mist went down there."

Rogan and McKenzie walked down to the sixth floor of the Amdahl hotel. Back in its day, this hotel was the go-to spot for celebrities, the rich and famous, and anyone with a taste for the finer things in life. Now, decades later, after neglect and urban decay, the Amdahl hotel served an entirely different clientele, one that preferred to pay by the hour. The gold diamond carpets with the red-fringed edges were stained, worn, and crusted over with any number of things, and the antique plaster walls, the life's work of a great artisan, were crumbled and smeared with spray paint and paint remover.

Multitudes of grizzly events occurred at the Amdahl during its downward spiral, including seventeen unsolved murders and sixteen suicides. Eighteen of those untimely deaths happened on the sixth floor, the majority in room 616.

"We ready?" asked Rogan, walking into 617.

"Yeah, everything is set," replied Troll. Everyone he knew called him Troll, except his mother, who called him Travis. He always looked down on Rogan and Mac, not because he thought less of them, but because he was a solid foot taller than either of them. He got his broad shoulders and tree trunk legs from his years of champion wrestling in high school and college. When he wasn't lifting weights and pinning guys to the mat, Troll studied biology and world religions in college. He was also well on his way to earning his medical degree.

Troll had an odd fascination with the dead. Not only did he hunt ghosts for fun, he worked with dead bodies for a living as an assistant to the county coroner. His knowledge of strange and often forgotten religions, as well as his constant contact with the macabre, made Troll a valuable resource to the team. He was also a true believer in the paranormal, which nicely offset Rogan's skepticism.

"Angus, base is ready?"

"You know it, bro."

Angus Rin was an anomaly. His father was born in Japan and still could barely speak English. Somehow, he fell in love with and married a full-blooded Scottish lass; their union created Angus. Angus was half Scottish, half Japanese, and 100% awesome—or at least that's what he told girls at parties. From his father, Angus got his skin tone and a slight pronunciation of the eyes. From his mother, he got his demeanor, height, and brownish-red hair. Most people could not tell his nationality of origin from looks alone, and, instead of trying to explain it to them, Angus always told people he was American: nothing more, nothing less.

As far as Rogan was concerned, Angus was a bit of a wild card. Other than the haunts, Rogan had no idea what Angus did for a living, nor did he know where he lived. He didn't even know what type of soda Angus preferred. Angus Rin was, however, insanely good with technology, and somehow he always had the hook up to get a good deal. Angus served as the team's technical person. He stayed at the designated home base and made sure that everything recorded properly. He also set up all the cameras and outfitted the three investigators with their gear.

"Awesome, let's go dark then," said Rogan. Going dark usually meant cutting the power to the area to be investigated. They did this so that there would be no electrical interference that might mislead their sensors. While Rogan had been spinning around corners and throwing doors into people, Angus had set up an array of heat sensors, thermal cameras, video cameras, and EMP sensors in various locations on the sixth floor with the focus on room 616.

Unfortunately, they wouldn't be going completely dark. As much as the team tried to convince the current owners of the Amdahl that they were doing critical research, the owners refused to cut power to an entire floor of the hotel. Rogan was able to rent all the rooms on the floor, though, which meant the team should not have to worry about anything living messing with their equipment.

"Okay, recording?" asked Rogan. Troll nodded and pointed a camera at Rogan. "Good. Okay, welcome to P.I.T. case 16976-4, the Amdahl hotel. As always, I'm joined by my assistants Mac, Troll, and our tech guru, Angus."

P.I.T. stood for Paranormal Investigation Team. Rogan founded the team four years ago, and since then the four members had explored many haunted locations and re-searched people claiming to have paranormal abilities. They even took on an alien case once in a while. They recorded everything for posterity and posted it on their website. Once in a while they would even live stream the hunt, but not tonight.

"Mac, can you give us the rundown?"

"Sure, Rogan. The Amdahl has a pretty sketchy past. There have been almost twenty deaths to date in the hotel, most of them occurring on the sixth floor, which is where we are stand-ing. We are going to focus our investigation on the hotspot, room 616. There have been three suicides and five murders in this room alone. Visitors to the hotel report seeing a woman in white standing by the window. They also claim to hear a child crying in the bathroom. There are also reports of pictures tilt-ing or falling off the walls and lamps falling from tables. Rogan and I will head into 616 while Troll heads down to 619."

"Yeah, I'm going out solo to check out 619. Major blood bath in there. The story goes that three thieves robbed a bank and met back in the Amdahl to split the loot back in the 1920s. While they were splitting up their goods, a rival group of thieves broke in to rob the robbers. All six men ended up shooting one another in a crazy crossfire. Recent reports state that the lights flick off and on randomly in the room and that anything plugged in becomes unplugged. People report hear-ing men's voices arguing and the sound of gunshots," said Troll.

"Thanks, guys. We also have an array of motion sensors, thermal sensors, and recording devices in all the rooms on the sixth floor, as well as in the hallways. Alright, let's do this. Troll, good luck."

"Rogan and McKenzie entering 616. It is 2:15 am," said McKenzie.

"Hear you loud and clear," said Angus through the earpiece that all the team members wore.

Rogan opened the door to 616. He stepped into the room and headed to the right. The room was dark. Ominous shadows fell across the bed, flickering with the neon sign hanging outside. Rogan found comfort in the silence before a hunt. It was one of the few times he felt his constantly swirling mind come to a peaceful rest. Rogan and Mac silently walked the perimeter of the room, each pointing their handheld cameras everywhere they went.

"Rogan, I got something here."

"What is it, Mac?"

"Cold spot by the painting. It's a good five degrees colder than the air around it. Should we try to provoke?"

Rogan walked over to the spot where Mac was pointing her heat sensor gun. It did feel colder. He felt a tingle up his spine—maybe this was it. Was there something here, standing right next to him, something stuck between worlds?

"Well?" asked Mac.

"Air vent. You're pointing your gun at an air vent."

"Bummer..."

"Woah, look at the painting," said Rogan.

Rogan and Mac stared at the painting on the wall over the bed. It displayed a vase with a set of three yellow flowers. The frame was large, probably two feet by three feet. As they watched, the painting moved from being square to being askew, the lower right corner moving closer and closer to the headboard.

"That is beyond creepy," said McKenzie.

Rogan walked over to the wall and placed his hand next to the painting. He could feel a light rhythmic vibration. He knew that no one was in the room next door. Where was the vibration coming from? He looked up and noticed small bits of plaster dust drifting down from above.

"What is it?" asked McKenzie.

"I think a customer is hard at work upstairs. The vibration is coming down the wall and causing the painting to move. Angus, make a time mark, let's check with the front desk and see if the room above 616 is in use."

"Got it," said Angus.

"Wait, did you hear that?" asked Rogan.

"Yeah, like a whining noise, from the bathroom."

Rogan and Mac stood at either side of the bathroom door, like two cops ready to bust into a drug house. Rogan gave a silent three count and burst through the door, handi-cam drawn. They swept the small bathroom, but the sound was gone.

"You heard that, right?" asked Rogan.

"Yeah, it was like a kid sobbing."

"Okay you stay here and do an EVP session. I'm going to step out and see if Angus got anything on audio."

"I'll queue that spot up, bro," said Angus.

As Rogan walked towards the door of 616, he felt a familiar feeling crawl up his spine. The mist was back. He spun around looking for it. It was floating near the window, light as fog and as fragile as dandelion seeds floating on a spring wind. It hung motionless, backlit by the flickering neon sign.

"Tell me you're seeing this," said Rogan, bringing up his camera.

"Seeing what, man?" asked Angus.

"The floating apparition by the window?"

"You see it again?" called McKenzie.

"You saw it before?"

"Yeah in the hallway upstairs, long story."

McKenzie came out of the bathroom as the mist made its move for the door, dashing right through Rogan. He felt like a jet of frost had been shot through his chest. His legs wobbled and he fell to the floor.

"Are you okay?" yelled McKenzie as Rogan scrambled to his feet.

"Yeah, I'm going after her!"

"Her?"

Rogan ran out of 616 and down the hallway, this time slowing as he spun around the corner. He burst through the stairwell door and half ran, half fell down two flights of stairs. The mist continued through the door and down the hallway on the fourth floor. It hovered in front of door 416. From what Rogan could recall of his research on the Amdahl hotel, nothing paranormal had been reported on the fourth floor. Rogan approached the apparition. Just as he was about to reach out to the ghost, it disappeared through the door.

Rogan knocked on the door. "Hello, anyone in there?"

He waited a moment and knocked again, louder this time. He waited and then tried the door knob. It turned in his hand. He pushed the door open and stepped into one of the most horrifying scenes he had seen in all his days as a Paranormal Investigator.

A small light from the bedside table dimly lit the room. The smell hit him first, rancid meat mixed with an array of putrid aromas. This was not the first time he had smelled death, but it was certainly the worst time. He stared, transfixed, at the woman lying on the bed. She was naked, hands tied to the headboard, feet tied to the footboard. Her head was propped up on a pillow, allowing her dead, hollow eyes to stare directly at Rogan. He fought back the urge to vomit and covered his nose with a handkerchief from his pocket.

Above the headboard, behind the staring dead woman, was a message written in blood: *The Devil comes to take your Heart*. Rogan scanned down from the bloody message, back to the murdered woman. Her chest had been opened up like someone had found a treasure chest and simply opened the lid. Her ribs fanned out to her sides, forming a pair of boney hands surrounding the cavity. Rogan walked a few steps closer, and though he was not an expert in human anatomy, he could see that there was a big empty space where the heart should be.

"Why did she lead me here? Why did she want me to see this?"

"Rogan? Rogan…what are you talking about, bud? Where are you?" asked Troll, breaking Rogan from his trance.

"Hey, Troll, I forgot you were in my ear. We need to call 911. I found a body."

2.

Her favorite part of the day was the morning she held a cup of fresh-brewed coffee with sugar and watched the pink and lavender rays dance off the pond as the sun rose above the pines that lined the parking lot. Karin Gilmore used the single moment of serenity to center her mind. She readied her spirit for the day, standing there on the balcony overlooking the grounds, the robust scent of hot java wafting into her nostrils. Karin sighed as she looked at the buzzing pager clipped to her suede leather belt. *Almost thirty whole seconds*, she thought as she walked down the hall towards the chaos. Karin smiled and nodded toward each passing nurse, courier, and assistant as she strode towards the transplant unit.

"Karin, there you are. Can I talk to you a moment?"

"Well if you can walk and talk, Jim. I just received a page," replied Karin.

Dr. James Paige dropped in beside Karin, struggling to match her pace. Karin respected Dr. Paige as a doctor; he was one of the best transplant surgeons in the nation. He wasn't all-together bad looking either. Being in his mid-sixties, he was a little too old for Karin, but with his distinguished salt-and-pepper hair, a feature displaying his years of experience, and his athletic build, he was a handsome man. Still, something in his light blue eyes always gave her pause. Call it a woman's intuition, but Karin knew he was not always showing all his cards.

"I don't suppose it's a heart, by chance?"

"Kidneys, Doctor, why do you ask?"

"It's Hope in room 211. I'm afraid she is running out of time. We ran another battery of tests this morning, and she's declining rapidly," said Dr. Paige.

Hope was Karin's second favorite part of the day. Born with a malformed heart, she had spent more of her life inside the hospital than out. She was an amazing little girl. No one expected her to live more than two or three years, but she would soon celebrate her seventh birthday. Karin made it part of her day to visit each of the patients in the transplant ward, and though no one would ever wish for someone to be hospitalized, Karin loved seeing Hope. Her blonde locks and smiling face easily rivaled the rising sun and the glistening pond.

"I see. How bad is it?" asked Karin, stopping abruptly in the hall.

"We'll know more soon."

"Come on Jim, I'm not a patient, level with me."

"Without a transplant? Maybe another day or two. She can barely move as it is. It's just not right if you ask me. I know it's terrible to think, but it makes me hope for a tragic car crash."

Karin squeezed Dr. Paige's forearm. For all his eccentricities, he cared deeply for his patients. His eyes darkened as he looked down at her. Karin's amber eyes blinked back tears. The brief moment between concerned colleagues was broken by the buzzing at Karin's belt. Karin withdrew her hand and turned to head towards the receiving area.

"I'll stop by and see her after I deal with this," said Karin, pointing at her pager.

Karin picked up the pace, leaving Dr. Paige standing in the hall, her high heels clicking as she walked. She entered the receiving room to find an older gentleman holding a blue cooler. He held it out with a smile. The hospital employed a number of couriers to deliver a variety of things between different hospital campuses within the area. The couriers were almost always retired men who did not want to leave the workforce just yet.

After signing for the delivery, Karin took the cooler into the lab next door. She stood with her eyes closed for a moment and clutched the handle of the cooler. She silently prayed that there was a mix up and that she would find a viable heart inside instead of a set of kidneys.

She held her breath and slowly pulled the lid off of the cooler. She let her breath go in a loud sigh as she stared down at a perfect set of kidneys. Normally, she was excited to see new organs, because she knew it meant one of her patients would receive a chance at a longer life. Today though, she wanted a heart—she needed a heart—for Hope. She closed her eyes for a moment. She needed to refocus. Hope was not her only patient—today would be a lucky day for a couple of critical patients currently on dialysis. She shook her head as she lifted the small set of organs out of the medical cooler, forcing a smile to her face.

As the Transplant Coordinator for the hospital, it was Karin's job to take delivery of any incoming organs. Once she had an organ, she determined its viability and compared the results with the transplant list. When a match was found, she coordinated with the surgery department to complete the transplant. She found both kidneys to be viable and confirmed that they matched the transplant list. Then she got to do one of her favorite things. Karin picked up the phone and called the two patients that would receive the kidneys. She walked out of the lab with most of her good mood restored.

Another cup of coffee, and it was time for rounds. Karin purposely saved room 211 for last. She knocked on the door and entered the room to find Hope lying in bed coloring. As soon as Hope saw Karin, her baby blue eyes began to sparkle. The room smelled like all hospital rooms, sterile—a smell that Hope was unfortunately very used to. An old episode of Looney Toons whispered quietly from the TV. The rays of midmorning sun landed on Hope's goldenrod hair through the open blinds.

"Hi Karin! Look at what I colored," said Hope.

"Oh! Well, let me see!"

"It's a lion. I colored it for Dr. Paige. He seemed sad this morning."

"That was very nice of you, honey."

"He says I really need to get a heart. I told him not to worry. If I don't get a heart then I get to go to Heaven. That doesn't seem too bad. Did you know that no one is sick in Heaven, Karin?"

"Yes, sweetie. I did know that. What else did Dr. Paige have to say?" asked Karin, trying to hide the crack in her voice.

"He told me not to lose '*hope*.' He thinks he is so funny."

"Yes he does, doesn't he?" said Karin, giggling.

Karin sat with Hope for another half an hour, much longer than she visited with any of the other patients. Usually Karin left Hope's room feeling refreshed and full of joy, but today she felt different. She walked down the hall towards her office. She moved slowly, her heels barely registering a sound against the brick hospital walls. As she turned the final corner before entering the office area of the floor, she came across Dr. Paige.

"It just makes me so mad, Jim. Why, after suffering for so long, have her prayers not been answered?" asked Karin.

"I know, Karin. It isn't right. She's going to be seven next week. Seven years. That's hardly anything."

"I just wish there was something I could do for her, but I can't magically produce a heart, and certainly not one that will match her genetic markers. But, like my dad always said, we have to have the strength to let go of that which we cannot control."

"Or find a way to control it…" said Dr. Paige as he walked away.

3.

Three cups of coffee into his day, and Richard Rogan still could not get the gory murder scene out of his mind. He had seen many dead bodies and countless murder scenes, but he'd never seen anything like that. The scene had a ritualistic feel to it—the woman was not simply murdered, but sacrificed. What was the point?

The nearly translucent apparition also took up residence in his mind. What was it? A trick of the eyes? Light playing off the mirrors and crystal ceiling lights of the Amdahl Hotel? Rogan fully embraced the fact that ghosts exist. However, he spent most of his time disproving haunted locations and stories of the paranormal. The apparition was one of the few things he could not explain.

Rogan's paranormal investigation team had a library of un-explainable sounds, smells, and feelings, but they had never documented visual proof of the paranormal beyond shifting shadows and glimmers from the corners of eyes. Rogan kicked himself for not capturing the apparition on film as Edna, the waitress at Rogan's favorite diner, delivered his daily breakfast of three pancakes and blueberry syrup. Rogan maintained an office located across the street from The Diner. The configuration of long-dead neon bulbs hung across the side of the narrow building simply stated Diner.

The restaurant clung to the 1950s with its cracking green stools, pastel green counter tops, and dense-foam, oversized booths. Edna, an older woman, likely wore the same pink-checked, frilly uniform today that she wore the day she started working at The Diner thirty years prior. She half shuffled, half walked away from Rogan's table without a word, holding a wrinkled hand to her lower back. Through the small window set in the wall behind the counter, Rogan could hear Delores, the pancake maker, humming out bars of Amazing Grace.

Rogan sat staring intently at the indentation on the seat across from him as he ate his blueberry syrup-soaked pancakes. Between bites, he sat back and twirled the large gold ring he wore on his right ring finger. The ring had a giant R, for Rogan, pressed into each side. On the crown of the ring, two fish chased each other in a circle, each nearly biting the others tail. The ring had been his father's; he never took it off.

The door creaked open as Rogan finished off his first cake. A slender woman walked in, clutching her elbows. She scanned the long, narrow room with her head angled towards the black-and-white tiled floor. She was younger than Rogan, in her early twenties by his best guess. A simple white tank top draped lazily over her boney shoulders. A pair of cutoff jean shorts hung just above her knees. Her brown eyes continued to scan the room as she took a hand from her elbow to run a set of long slender fingers through her unkempt, wispy blonde hair. She walked deeper into the diner. Rogan glanced up from his breakfast, catching her sad brown eyes as she came to a stop next to his table.

"Ex-excuse me. I don't mean to bother, but are you Richard Rogan?"

Rogan swallowed hard and stared directly at the young woman. She bit her lip.

"A cop told me I could find him here. Richard Rogan that is," she continued.

Rogan calmly placed his fork down on top of the pale green tabletop.

"He said you eat here every morning—you have every morning for long as he can remember."

Rogan did eat at The Diner nearly every day, extenuating circumstances aside. It wasn't for the pancakes, which were average at best. It wasn't for the syrup, which was from a commercial bottle. It certainly wasn't for the conversion with tho attentive wait staff.

"My…my sister died last night at the Amdahl. I found your card in the hallway."

Rogan had left his card with a Detective, or at least someone who fancied himself one. Detective Rodriguez and Rogan had a sordid history. Rogan could picture Rodriguez flippantly discarding his card as Rogan walked away.

"The cop said you found her body. I was hoping I could talk to you. Can I sit?"

The woman started to lower her small frame into the seat across from Rogan. Rogan's eyes enlarged as her form approached the large indent in the foam.

"No! I mean, yes, but please don't sit there," said Rogan. "Let's sit in the next booth, and you can tell me why you tracked me down."

Rogan stood to his full six and a quarter feet, and he and his pancakes moved one booth further from the door. The woman followed, taking a seat across from Rogan. She looked more than a little perplexed.

"What's your name?" asked Rogan.

"Darla. Why did we have to move?"

"Oh, it's just that seat is really uncomfortable with that big old indent."

"Well that makes sense, I suppose," she said, looking at him questionably.

"So Darla, since you are crashing my daily pancakes, you might as well eat with me. My treat."

She smiled and glanced over the menu. Given her gaunt appearance, it was clear to Rogan that she did not typically eat three squares a day. Darla placed her order with the always-silent Edna and began to sip on a warm cup of black coffee.

"Care to tell me why you hunted me down while you wait for your food?"

"Is it true that, you know, you found her?"

"Yes, that is true."

"The cops wouldn't let me see her body. Just her face. What happened to her? I'm tough—I can take it"

"To be honest, I have no idea. I've never seen anything quite like it. Whatever happened in that room, it was not your typical homicide."

"Did you see the writing on the wall?"

"Yes. Yes I did."

"Good. I was wondering if you would look into it for me? I don't have much money, but I would find a way to pay you. I have to know what happened."

"Darla, I'm afraid I don't investigate murders anymore. That life has passed me by. It would be best for you to work with the police."

"But your card. It says you are a P.I."

"Which I am. I'm a Paranormal Investigator."

"Exactly. That's why I need you to look into this."

Rogan gaped at her, syrup dripping from his fork. He raised his right eyebrow and stared at the small blonde girl tightly gripping her coffee mug.

"Isn't it obvious, Mr. Rogan? A demon did this…"

"Darla, I was a police officer for a number of years, and while I believe in the paranormal, I can assure you that the only real demons in this world are human."

Even though he had never captured concrete proof, Rogan believed in ghosts, poltergeists, and any number of things that have a proclivity to go bump in the night. However, Rogan had spent enough time as a homicide detective to know that real violence, the kind we should all fear, is not the work of demons or devils, but people. Brothers, sisters, parents, friends, and loved ones are slaughtered, not by a red man with pointy horns and a trident, but by brothers, sisters, parents, friends, and loved ones.

"My Grandma used to tell me and Tammy that if we strayed from the path the Devil would come to claim our hearts," said Darla, staring into Rogan's green eyes. "Don't you see, you have to help me. You used to solve murders. My sister was murdered. Now you hunt ghosts. I know her killer was something weird. Just like Grandma said. Please Mr. Rogan, please help me."

Darla dropped her head into her hands and sobbed. Tears dropped onto the table. Rogan reached into his pocket and pulled out a clean cotton handkerchief. He handed it to Darla. She sat back against the booth, giving a small, difficult smile to Rogan. She dabbed the tears from her face. She twisted the handkerchief in her hands as she rested her forearms on the edge of the booth.

"Mr. Rogan, you know as well as I do that no matter what happened to my sister, no one is going to spend any time trying to figure it out. No one is going to care that another hooker died in the Basin. Please..."

Rogan stared into her brown eyes, watching tears well and drip from the corners of her eyelids. He needed to help her.

Rogan quit the force when his sister died in the line of duty. She was also a detective—a much *better* detective, in Rogan's opinion. Their father used to be the Police Chief, and their grandfather died a Captain. Their great-grandfather still held the record for most arrests in a single day. The first sheriff of Queen City bore the surname Rogan. The blue blood of law enforcement ran through the generations—only to dry up with Richard Rogan. He was the last of the namesake, but after the consecutive deaths of his mother, father, and sister, all of whom died while in the duty of the police department, Rogan hung up his cuffs. Today marked the first time since he had left the force some five years prior that he felt compelled to investigate something that would likely end up being non-paranormal.

Rogan stared into Darla's pleading eyes and sighed. He was coming out of retirement.

4.

Karin spent the next hour arranging surgeries for the two thankful patients who were in need of new kidneys. Helping the patients and seeing the elation on their faces kept Hope out of Karin's mind for the moment. When she entered into the medical world, Karin knew that she would have to deal with death and loss. She knew that no matter how hard she tried, or how many hours she put in, she could not possibly save everyone that walked through the doors. Most of the time she accepted that fact, but cases like Hope's rocked her faith.

She walked down the halls of the transplant wing, glancing in the rooms as she went. She tried not to think about who she would lose next. Nearing the corner before her office, she saw the grandfather of one of the patients stepping out into the hall. He was a wonderful man named Winston. He came to visit every single day. His daughter had been a closet drug addict. While she was pregnant with Jenny, she sniffed, snorted, and stuck just about anything she could get her hands on into her body. The influx of narcotics caused Jenny to be born extremely premature. Miraculously, she survived, but her mother died in childbirth.

The drugs also caused Jenny to have a number of birth defects, including a heart with deformed chambers. She had made it eleven years with the bad heart. As her body grew, though, the smaller-than-normal chambers had become an issue. Now her only option would be to get a donor heart.

Winston was an older man, gracefully bald, with tightly shaved gray wings over his ears that met behind his head. He always had a smile on his face, with crow's feet wrinkles leading out from his gentle brown eyes. Karin couldn't help but wonder what he must have been like back in his prime.

"Karin, how are you today?"

"I'm getting along. How are you, Winston?"

"I'm okay, though I'd be doing better if you had some news?"

"I'm afraid I don't. As you know, your granddaughter has a couple rare genetic markers. We have our net stretched out as far as we can, but so far no matches. We won't stop looking, though. You know that."

"Yes, I do. I'll just keep hoping. Dr. Paige tells me that she may not have a great deal more time."

Winston's soft brown eyes fell to the floor, and his usual smiling countenance disappeared. Karin could tell that he loved his granddaughter more than anything. She was the only family he had, and he was the only family she had. Karin also knew that Winston was not well. He had been diagnosed with lymphatic cancer. The prognosis was not good. The cancer was inoperable and spreading—it could take him under any day.

"This may sound morbid, but I hope I go first."

"Oh, Winston, don't think like that. We aren't going to lose either one of you."

Karin said it, but she didn't believe it. Winston would lose his fight soon; cancer like his was too aggressive to beat. She did believe they would find a heart for Jenny, though. She had some rare genetic needs, but not so rare that it would be impossible.

"They must teach you to say things like that in medical school these days, I suppose?" asked Winston, some of his smile returning.

"No, they don't, and I've been out of school a long time."

"You don't look it, my dear."

"Always the flirt," said Karin, slapping Winston playfully on the arm.

"Dr. Paige gives her a week, maybe two on the high side."

"That gives us a week to find her a heart. We will find one, Winston. You just have to believe."

"It's getting hard, but I'll try. Off to my treatment now. Good day, dear."

Winston walked off towards the Cancer Center. Karin stood in the hall for a moment watching him go. She guessed he was seventy, or maybe even seventy-five. He always walked with a slight shuffle. His body was giving out from the cancer, but Karin had not met many people with a sharper mind.

Once Winston travelled beyond the set of double doors at the end of the hall, Karin turned towards her office. She was determined to make as many calls as necessary to find a heart for Jenny. She opened the door to her office and, much to her surprise, saw a small blue medical cooler sitting on the center of her oak desk. It was not unheard of to have multiple organs delivered on the same day, but it was unheard of to have them sitting on her desk.

She grabbed the pager from her belt; she had not missed a page. She went over to her computer. The kidneys were the only delivery scheduled for today. If it was an emergency, she would have been paged. All incoming organs were to go to the receiving room to be processed in a sterile environment.

She picked up her phone and began to dial the courier's office to find out how this cooler ended up on her desk and why. Halfway through dialing, she put the phone down. She picked up the cooler and turned it. Looking at it carefully, she could tell it was definitely a medical cooler, but it had no paperwork pouch. Usually when an organ arrived, it had a small bundle of paperwork folded into a small plastic pouch glued to the side of the cooler. Karin would take this paperwork and match it up with the electronic copy on her computer to confirm that the organ matched. This organ had no paperwork, and it was sitting on her desk. Curiosity got the best of her. Karin picked up the cooler and walked down to the receiving lab.

Karin put on the appropriate sterile garb and opened the cooler. Sitting in the bottom of the cooler, set perfectly on top of transport ice, was a heart. She quickly closed the lid and looked around the room. She was alone. Karin walked over to the nearest computer and pulled up the transplant registry.

There were no hearts scheduled to be delivered. Nor did anything show up in the list of organs to be distributed.

She decided there would be no harm in testing the viability of the organ, so she ran the heart through the normal testing protocol. She impatiently tapped her fingers on the desk while the computer worked on the data. A minute later the printer came to life, printing out the report of the heart's viability. Karin read through the report, gasped, and ran back to the computer. She pulled up the hospital's transplant list and compared the test results. The heart matched nearly perfectly with one patient—Hope.

Karin spent the next five minutes pacing back and forth. There were strict policies in place regarding organ donation and transplantation. All organs had to be registered and distributed by the central registry. The centralized system served as a way to deter black market or illegally-harvested organs, which meant that Karin was bound by her duties to reject this heart and report the issue. She found herself trapped in a conundrum. On one hand, she had a perfect heart for Hope. On the other hand, she had no idea where it came from. If anyone found out that she had accepted an unregistered organ, she would lose her job. She could deal with losing her job, but then she wouldn't be able to help the other kids waiting for transplants. Hope only had a day or two to live; this heart could be her last chance. She continued to pace and chew on her nails. The lab phone rang, jerking her out of her thoughts.

"This is Dr. Gilmore."

"Karin! There you are. We have a situation I thought you would want to know," said Susan, one of the transplant nurses.

"What is it, Susan?"

"Hope went into cardiac arrest a couple minutes ago. Dr. Paige got her stabilized, but he doesn't think she'll come back next time. He said I should call you, so you could say goodbye if you want."

Karin held the phone to her chest, tears welling in her eyes. Karin believed in signs, and she believed in destiny. This could not be any clearer. She had made her decision.

"Susan, tell Dr. Paige to prep for surgery."

After breakfast, Rogan took a taxi down to the Basin. The taxi dropped him off in front of the famous Amdahl hotel, which recently added another murder to its reputation. Rogan looked up at the fourth floor. He could see the window covered with yellow crime scene tape. He put his hands in his black trench coat and wrapped the jacket tightly around him as he walked through the lobby doors.

Rogan could vaguely remember the way the Amdahl lobby used to look. He used to eat at the Amdahl with his parents on weekends. They stopped going when he was about seven—by then, the urban decay had taken over the hotel. The Sunday brunch buffet shut down as the hotel transformed from a place for families and debutantes to a place for drug dealers and prostitutes.

Rogan remembered staring up at the gigantic crystal chandelier every time the Rogan family walked in after church, but the beautiful crystal had disappeared many years ago. The gold-accented front desk had been replaced with a metal desk surrounded by bulletproof glass. Rogan walked past the desk to the stairwell. The Amdahl had elevators, and many patrons used them, but considering the complete disregard for safety and maintenance Rogan had seen while exploring the old hotel, he had no intention of becoming one of its ghostly guests. He stuck to the stairs.

Once on the fourth floor, Rogan walked to room 416. Yellow tape crisscrossed the span of the doorway. A sign hung prominently on the door, indicating that no one should enter. Rogan ignored the warnings and reached for the doorknob. The door, not surprisingly, was locked. Rogan pulled a lock picking set from the inner pocket of his coat. In a matter of seconds he heard a satisfying click as he worked the slender tools in the lock. With a push, the door swung open, revealing the dark crime scene. Rogan stepped through one of the diamonds formed by the crime scene tape and entered the room. The air still smelled flush with the unmistakable scent of drying blood. The body was gone, but a clear red outline remained where Tammy had died.

Rogan began working the scene the way his father had taught him so many years ago. Start on the outside, work your way towards the body. He walked the perimeter of the room looking for anything the Crime Scene Unit may have missed. Rogan continued in slow semi-circles towards the bed. The Crime Scene Unit had been thorough. Residue of finger print powder covered every surface. The carpet had obviously been vacuumed. They would search through the particles looking for clues about the killer. Rogan shivered thinking about what they may have vacuumed out of this carpet. Rogan looked up again at the message: *"The Devil comes to collect your heart."* He got close to it, smelled it, and then touched it. Something wasn't right. He took a small flashlight from his inner jacket pocket and aimed it at the message, moving the light beam back and forth across the letters. As he moved the light, the letters shimmered back.

"It's paint," he said aloud as he continued to stare at the words.

Rogan turned to the bed. *From the outside in*, he thought, and ran his hand along the bed frame, feeling between the frame and the well-worn box spring mattress.

"Ouch" he yelped and pulled his hand out about halfway down the length of the frame. Rogan lifted his hand to find a hypodermic needle sticking out of the side of his hand. His initial reaction was to pull it out, which would have been a good idea. Instead, he stumbled backwards over the nightstand. Rogan fell onto the recently-vacuumed shag carpeting, landing on his side. His hand slammed into the floor, pressing the plunger on the syringe, which sent a shot of liquid under his skin.

"Shit…shit…shit," said Rogan, scrambling to his feet.

As soon as he managed to stand, he fell again to his knees. He felt his eyelids getting heavy. Before he lost all ability to think, he pulled out this mobile phone and called Mac.

"What Rogan? I'm trying to enjoy a well-deserved morning of sleeping in."

"I have a little problem."

"You have more than one, and none of them are little."

"Funny…look I don't have much time. I think I'm going to pass out. Can you call Sam and have her come get me at the Amdahl?"

"Why, what did you do?"

"Nothing, just call her, okay. She'll find me on the fourth floor, Hur…."

Rogan stumbled towards the door, no longer able to speak. He felt like his mind was bouncing off the sides of his skull. He could only manage to keep one of his eyes open, and then only to a mere slit. After one more awkward step forward, Rogan slammed face-first through the yellow tape across the doorway and landed half in the hallway. Rogan coughed as dust plumed up around his limp body, and then all went black.

5.

A steady beat of beeps and blips filled Rogan's ears as he came to. He slowly peeled his eyes open and took in his surroundings. His recently wounded left hand rested on his stomach, wrapped in beige bandages. The steady beep, beep, beep came from his right. He tried to raise his right hand towards the sound, but could not lift it from under the blanket. *Must be asleep,* he thought as he looked around. Scanning to his left he found Mac, curled up in an uncomfortable-looking chair. Her slender legs were pulled tightly into her chest, her long arms wrapped around her legs. Her forehead was smushed into the top of her knees, leaving her bright red hair to drape to the top of her calves. She looked so peaceful—a peaceful, sleeping ball.

Rogan watched her sleep for a moment while he waited for his mind to catch up. He had known Mac nearly his entire life. She started coming over to the Rogan house to play with his sister, Sarah, when they were seven, which made Mac just four years old. She endlessly chased Sarah around the

Rogan's craftsman style home, freckles and pigtails bouncing down the halls. Back then she always wore dresses, and she usually had one or both of her stockings bunched up around her ankles. Sometimes Rogan missed the dresses and freckles. Mac would not be caught dead in a dress today, and she outgrew her freckles in high school.

Mac's family lived around the corner. Because she lived close, and because she didn't have any brothers or sisters, she came to visit often. Sarah, however, never went around the corner to visit McKenzie. McKenzie's mom was a drug addict. A very sneaky, clever drug addict, but a user just the same. Mac's dad had run off when she was born, leaving her wreck of a mother to care for the newborn.

Caring for someone else was not something Mac's mother excelled at, so Rogan's parents unofficially adopted the tiny fireball. She ate supper with the family almost every night and often slept there when her mom couldn't be bothered to be home. Rogan's dad even built a set of bunk beds in Sarah's room. Rogan always wondered why his police parents didn't bust Mac's mom. When Rogan was older and attending the police academy he asked his dad that very question. He remembered the conversation verbatim.

"Son, sometimes doing it right, ain't right. You need to remember that when you get out in the real world. What do you think would have happened if we would have busted McKenzie's mother?"

"She would have gone to jail," Rogan replied.

"That's right, but what would have happened to McKenzie?"

Rogan furrowed his brow and looked up at his father, who wore the same smirk and eye twinkle he always had when he knew he was about to teach his son some deep, worldly lesson.

"Well?"

"I don't know."

"Exactly."

"What are you talking about, Dad?"

"Think about it, son. We bust her mom for doing rocks, and what happens? Little McKenzie gets shipped off to some foster family, bounces around the system, and who knows. Your mother and I decided it was better to turn a blind eye so we could keep a good eye on McKenzie, make sure she had a family that cared about her."

Rogan thought about that concept as he watched the peaceful McKenzie ball contract and expand with every sleeping breath. The truth of his father's words had been proven time and again in his life. *Sometimes doing it right, ain't right. Rules to live by.*

"Mac?" Rogan said hoarsely.

The ball uncurled and McKenzie leapt out of the chair, caught her foot on the chair leg and slammed nose first into Rogan's stomach.

"You okay?" asked Rogan.

"Yeah I'm fine, sorry about that."

"It's okay. Am I okay?"

"What? Oh yeah, you're fine. They are still running a couple tests to make sure you didn't catch anything from the needle."

"What the heck was in that needle? It knocked me out in short order," asked Rogan.

"Some sort of powerful sedative. Gives me the shivers thinking about why a perve would have a syringe full in that place."

Rogan had a hypothesis forming about the syringe. It was looking less likely that Darla's sister had fallen victim to a demon attack. Someone had left that syringe behind on accident. Rogan felt certain that the needle was somehow connected to the murder. If the syringe contained a sedative, it would stand to reason that the killer used it to subdue his victim. Though Rogan could not yet figure out why the killer would subdue rather than kill, assuming that the sedative had been administered in room 416.

"What were you doing there anyway?" asked McKenzie.

"Investigating," replied Rogan.

"Investigating what?"

"The paranormal, of course."

"In room 416?"

"Yes, our client seems to think that her sister was killed by a demon."

"Our client?"

"Yes, Darla, the deceased's sister. She hired me this morning."

"We have clients?"

It was a fair question. Rogan had been a Paranormal Investigator for four years, but in that time he had never been hired to investigate anything. Instead, P.I.T. initiated an investigation after hearing stories about a location or paranormal activity.

"So, we are actually going to get paid?"

Another fair question. P.I.T never actually made any money; in fact, it was a very poor investment. Rogan did not care. He loved investigating the paranormal, no matter the lack of profits. After the rapid deaths of everyone in his family, Rogan inherited a great deal of money from pensions and life insurance policies, in addition to a large sum of money that his parents left to him in their will. Rogan was not a frivolous man. If he spent any of his family's money, it was for good reason.

"We'll be paid in the pride we'll feel after a job well done."

McKenzie tipped her head forward and rolled her eyes above the lenses of her dark-rimmed glasses. She was wearing her ever-present black hooded sweatshirt with its magenta piping and zipper. Rogan knew that she didn't buy his story. He wouldn't bo able to keep the ruse up for long. Still, Rogan did not want to admit to McKenzie that he was out solving murders again. Five years ago, after his sister died, Rogan swore he would never again do police work. McKenzie had been a strong supporter of that decision, so he wasn't sure how she would react to the news that he was coming out of retirement. He also knew that McKenzie had a big heart hidden behind her thick veil of sarcasm. One look at Darla's face this morning and she would have begged Rogan to help. Rogan's mind wandered back to the needle. It was his only lead at this point.

"Mac, can you call a nurse? I'd like to find out when I can get out of here and why I can't lift my right hand."

"Sure," said McKenzie pushing the call button on the bed. "I can shed some light on that arm thing, though."

McKenzie walked around the bed and pulled back the blanket covering Rogan's right arm. He looked down, shocked to see a silver bracelet connecting his wrist to the bed's side rail.

"Mac... Why the hell am I handcuffed to this bed?"

"Well..."

Rogan stared at her as she sheepishly glanced around the room. If her hair would have been pulled back into pigtails, she would have been a dead ringer for her five-year-old self. She only looked like that when she felt like she did something wrong or incredibly stupid. Rogan wondered which one this would be.

"You put me in kind of a bad position, calling me like that. So really it's your fault. Remember how you called me and then passed out in that gross old hotel?"

Rogan nodded.

"Well, I did like you said and called Sam, but she's on vacation, so her work phone was off. I panicked and made the situation kind of bad, though, technically, like I said, it's your fault for putting me in a bad spot."

"What did you do?"

"I may have panicked. I mean you could have been dead for all I knew, so I called the only other person I could think of that I had in my contacts....Rodriguez."

The votes were in; her sheepish act could be attributed to incredible stupidity. Right on cue, Detective Rodriguez slunk into the room. He was a short man, at least in comparison to Rogan. Rodriguez kept his hair cut tight to his scalp, his solution for premature balding. He took great pride in his perfectly-trimmed and manicured mustache. In his long tan suede trench coat he came casually sauntering towards Rogan with an ear-to-ear smile on his lightly tanned face.

"I see the master detective is awake."

"What do you want, Rodriguez?"

"Me? Oh nothing really, I just stopped by to read you your rights."

"Excuse me?"

"Your rights. You know, your Miranda Rights. I know you've been out for a while, but anyone that watches television knows what 'your rights' means."

"I know what my rights mean, you jack wagon. I'm more wondering why you think you get to read them to me."

"Well, back in 1966, Ernesto Arturo Miranda was accused of a crime, and taken into…"

Before he could complete his taunt, Rogan lunged towards Rodriguez, grabbing onto his pale striped tie with his bandaged hand. With a quick downward motion Rogan yanked Rodriguez's head towards the bed railing. Rodriquez managed to jerk free just before the bridge of his nose made contact with the metal rail.

"Oh good. I can add assaulting a police officer to the list."

"What else is on that list?" asked McKenzie, looking down into the fire burning behind Rogan's emerald eyes.

"How about tampering with evidence, disturbing a crime scene, and, oh yeah, murder."

Rogan just stared at Rodriguez's smug face. He thought about taking another swipe at him, but Rodriguez had stepped back out of one-armed lunging range. Rogan thought Rodriguez was slow, dimwitted, vindictive, and a terrible example of a detective. But he also had a hard time believing that the man in his houndstooth patterned sports coat and blue jeans really thought Rogan had committed the murder.

"Seriously, Rod, you think Rogan had something to do with that? We were with him all night," said McKenzie.

"Actually that isn't true. As you may recall, we seized your dork gear for evidence, in case one of you ghost nerds caught something on film or audio that might help. Plus it was really funny watching Rogan's face while we seized all that junk. How much of your dad's money did all that cost anyway?"

Rogan went to take another swing at Rod Rodriguez, but McKenzie stalled him with a hand on his shoulder. Rogan had not committed murder the night before, but the thought crossed his mind now as he stared angrily at Rodriguez.

"Interesting thing. We had our tech guys go through all of it. Most of it was garbage, but it did give us a lead. Rogan's movements were unaccounted for, for about twenty minutes."

Rogan knew what time Rodriguez was referring to. Rogan had turned off his equipment when he chased the apparition. He could not remember what compelled him to turn it off. As a paranormal investigator, one would think that would be the single most important time to have your audio and visual equipment up and running.

Last night was not the first time he had seen the ghost. He kept his findings a secret; the idea molding in his mind was too crazy. No one would believe him. Whenever the misty shape appeared, Rogan chased it, hoping that he would catch it. He hoped that if he could catch the spirit he might prove to himself that he was not entirely out of his mind.

"Why did you have your gear off?" asked McKenzie.

Rogan turned towards her to respond, but before he got a word in, Detective Rodriguez chimed in. "Et, no, not yet. Not a peep out of you. I want to make absolutely sure that anything stupid you are about to say can be used in a court of law."

Rodriguez began reading Rogan his rights. Before he could get one sentence in, Rogan interrupted. "Where's Sam? Shouldn't she be here keeping a leash on you?"

"I'm afraid Samantha is on vacation. You'll just have to make sad puppy dog eyes at me instead."

Samantha Stone was Rodriguez's partner and an excellent detective, with an impressive number of solved cases notched on her belt. Rogan stared at the door wishing he would see her long blonde ponytail bounce confidently into the room behind her focused steel blue eyes.

Rodriquez again started reciting the Miranda Rights. Rogan knew it by memory; he had said it himself countless times, though that seemed like ages ago. This, unfortunately, would not be the first time he had them recited to him. Somehow they sounded different when he was the speaker; there was always a feeling of triumph when the words entered his ears. On the receiving end, he felt sadness and anger. Even though he knew he was innocent, Rodrigeuz had a knack for spinning a good tale, and he could easily cast suspicion in Rogan's direction. Rogan could only hope that he hadn't burned all of his bridges with his former brothers and sisters in blue.

"I know you are dumb, but you aren't dumb enough to think Rogan had anything to do with this. Rod, you are such a vindictive prick," yelled McKenzie, interrupting Rodriguez once again.

"Seriously, I almost had it done that time."

Rogan turned to McKenzie and gave her a wink, a nonverbal thank you. The history between Rogan and Rodriguez stemmed back to one central issue, Rogan's sister. When Rogan and Sarah joined the force, Rodriguez served as Sarah's training officer. A relationship formed and subsequently dissolved. Rogan saw the whole thing as an older man in a position of power seducing his sister, and he made sure everyone, including his sister, knew it. Rodriguez blamed the relationship's sudden end on Rogan. He felt that Rogan, the overprotective brother, sabotaged the budding romance. The two had been both figuratively and physically at each other's throats ever since. Even after Sarah's tragic death, neither of the stubborn men let go of their anger. If anything, his sister's shooting fueled the fire more. Rogan blamed Rodriguez for sending them on the call without backup, even though he knew the risks. Rodriguez blamed Rogan for not protecting Sarah. He'd even gone so far as to say that Rogan should have been the one to take a bullet that night.

"Well Rod, are you going to answer the lady?" asked Rogan. "She is pretty young. Young enough for you, anyway. Maybe you want to ask her out for a drink instead."

"Don't think I don't know what you two are trying to do," said Rodriguez.

"And what's that, Rod?"

"You're trying to buy time. I'm sure Red over there called the old guy already."

"And who exactly are you calling old?" asked a deep voice from the doorway.

"Sir! No one, sir. Just trying to read this murder suspect his rights."

"Is that so?"

A tall, muscular, dark-skinned man filled the doorway of the hospital room. Rogan smiled at the man as he stepped into the room. Lazarus Cooper was the one bridge Rogan could always count on. Police Chief Lazarus Cooper earned his large barrel chest and matching arms through a lifetime of hard work. Police Chief Cooper started lifting weights when he was twelve years old, and he had not missed a single day in the gym in over 55 years. Even nearing 70 years of age, Co-op, as most people called him, was more physically fit and muscular than the new recruits entering the police force. His imposing figure earned him a lot of respect, as did his fair judgment and razor intelligence.

"And what evidence do you have, Detective?"

"Well, Chief, he was there last night."

"So were a lot of other people."

"For about twenty minutes his movements could not be accounted for."

"So were a lot of other people's."

"He was found tampering with the crime scene. It's my conclusion that he went back to cover his tracks. As you know, many criminals return to the scene."

"Rogan?" asked Coop.

"My client feels that her sister was murdered by a demon. I was just looking for evidence to support her claim."

"And did you find any?"

Rogan thought back to the needle and the fact that the message was written in red paint and not blood. He knew the contents of that needle were important, but he did not yet know why.

"Not to support the demonic angle, no, but I didn't have much time."

"Detective, when you arrived, what did you find to be tampered with?"

"He found a needle. It's my belief that he was trying to dispose of it before we found it, sir."

"Detective, please leave us."

"Yes sir," said Rodriguez, backing out of the room.

"Thanks for coming, Coop," said Rogan.

"I promised your father I always would, but dang it, Rogan, you make it hard for me to keep that promise."

After his father died in the name of duty, Coop filled the role of father figure for Rogan. Much to Rogan's surprise, Coop became one of Rogan's biggest supporters when he decided to leave the force. Coop told him that the Rogans were cursed and figured it might as well be Richard that ended it. For as long as the Rogans had served in Law Enforcement, Rogans had died protecting law and order. Richard Rogan did not have a single ancestor that had retired or died of old age. Almost all of them had taken a bullet while on duty. With the ground still loose over the graves of his immediate family, Rogan had made the decision to end the curse. He walked into Cooper's office, placed his gun and badge down, turned and walked out of the building.

Rogan had loved being a detective. He felt like he was doing work that meant something. He brought closure to families that had lost loved ones, but losing his own loved ones had proven to be too much. Rogan did the quick drop off in Cooper's office because he felt confident that Cooper would try to talk him out of it. Deep down, Rogan wished he had. The last five years of hunting ghosts and debunking the paranormal had been fun, but Rogan felt a consuming emptiness. The emptiness grew with each passing year. Now, lying in the hospital bed knowing that he was on a case, a real case, trying to find answers for Darla, the void felt ever-so-slightly filled.

"What in the name of heck were you doing poking around that crime scene, Richie?" said Coop. "And don't be giving me some talk about looking for ghosts."

Rogan began to open his mouth, then thought better of it and closed it. He needed a moment to think about what to say to the big man staring down at him with those penetrating brown eyes. After Rogan abruptly quit, Coop tracked him down at The Diner. Rogan expected that Coop would try to talk him into staying a detective. He did not so much fear the talk. He knew that it would only take a slight nudge to make him change his mind and pick up that gold shield again. Surprisingly though, Coop did not attempt to talk Rogan back. Instead he congratulated him on making a smart decision.

"I know you don't think a ghost did that to that poor girl, Richie. What are you up to?" asked Coop.

Rogan leaned out past the man towards the hospital room door. He could not see anyone lurking. Rogan leaned back into his pillow and sighed.

"Well Coop, the sister came to see me."

"So?"

"She was real shaken up. Said she thought a demon took her sister's heart."

"We both know that other than personal, demons don't exist, Rogan," said McKenzie, crossing her arms.

"You aren't helping," replied Rogan.

"And the boy does need help, young lady."

"Listen, I didn't think it was a demon, but she told a very compelling story about her grandmother. She used to tell Darla and her sister that if they strayed from the path of good, the devil would come collect their hearts."

"And in your 'professional' opinion, Richie, is that what happened, the devil came to get his due?"

"Well I hadn't completed my investigation..."

"Bullshit. You can't lie to me son, never could. Spill it."

Rogan took a breath and looked up at Coop. He watched as Coop flexed and released his massive biceps. Left, right, left, right, left, right. The rhythmic muscle flexing was an unconscious habit, a tell that Coop was agitated. Rogan did not want to tell Coop that he had been investigating the murder. He didn't know how the big man would react, but he was certain it wouldn't be good. Rogan had made a promise that he was done fighting crime—a promise that Coop was happy to accept. Lazarus Cooper never married, never had kids of his own, so for better or worse, Rogan was the closest thing to family he had. Richard Rogan also knew that no matter how hard he tried to fight it, his last name was Rogan and Rogan blood burned to solve crimes. He had suppressed it for five years, telling himself that debunking hauntings and charlatans was enough, but it wasn't. Even before Darla came to him, Rogan was working the crime in his mind, envisioning scenarios and forming ideas of how to proceed. All he needed was a push, which Darla provided. Time to man up...

"She told me that the police wouldn't care about some dead hooker. You and I both know she's right. I told her I would find out what really happened, and I intend to."

Coop sighed deeply, his barrel chest straining the buttons on his shirt. His dancing biceps slowed and eventually stopped. He looked at the floor for a moment and turned his dark eyes to Rogan.

"I'll have Rodriguez drop the murder charge. We all know it wasn't you. I am, however, going to have him book you on intentionally disturbing a crime scene. Hopefully a night sitting in the cage will remind you of why you gave up this life.

Lazarus Cooper turned on his heel and walked towards the door.

"Why do you care if I help this girl?" asked Rogan.

Coop stopped, shook his head, and continued walking out the door. A few moments later, Rodriguez strode in, smiling.

6.

He couldn't believe how good he felt.

His work was important. He knew that what he was doing would change lives. There was always a price. To give life, he would have to take life. Before enacting his mission he had never killed. He wasn't sure how he would react. Now he did.

He felt powerful.

He smiled up at the few stars visible through the array of street lights and neon in the Basin. He had worried about the pieces of the puzzle he couldn't control. He wasn't sure that Karin would play along. Turns out she played along perfectly. It helped that the first heart was for her favorite patient, and that patient mysteriously took a sudden turn for the worse. It also helped that he had an extensive knowledge of medicine.

He crossed the street to the Amdahl hotel, hoping that his disguise would work again. He wondered if it was too forward to kill another girl in the same place. He walked confidently into the lobby. There she was, sitting on one of the disheveled couches. He liked the Amdahl—it reminded him of his younger days. He remembered bringing more than a couple lovely ladies to this very hotel back in his prime. Back then, though, he didn't have to pay for it. He turned his head away from the front desk, walking past the couches. She looked up at him, pretty, brown eyes, long legs. He nodded, and she smiled. Yellow teeth. It took her a second to stand up on her long boots with large, chunky heels. He followed her boots up with his eyes, a small piece of tanned skin showed and then a tight leopard print dress began, leading him up to her cleavage.

She walked and took his arm. He liked that. Used to be a man and woman would always walk that way. Now the man is checking sports scores on his phone, and she's a foot away, staying in touch with the latest digital gossip. He didn't trust the elevators, but at his age, he would have to deal with it. He did not want to be winded when they got up to the fifth floor. He had rented the room directly above the room he had been in the previous evening. He wondered if anyone would notice.

She was chewing gum and smelled like strawberries. Her curly brown hair fell across her shoulders. It smelled of chemicals. He wondered when they would invent hairspray that smelled good. The elevator clicked and clattered upwards. He let his hand slid down her back and on to her rear. He gave it a slight squeeze. She smiled at him with supple red lips. He wished they were there for other reasons. He would have enjoyed her. Unfortunately, that part of his anatomy had failed him years ago, and even the advances in science did not help. He blamed his days as a cyclist. He used to race semi-professionally when he was younger to make ends meet. Plus he loved the competition.

The elevator dinged, announcing its arrival. He sighed, relieved to have made another trip up without catastrophe. She stepped off the elevator first, and he followed, pointing the way. They arrived at room 516. He opened the door and motioned her in. She looked around the room like she had never been there before, which seemed unlikely, based on her reputation. He watched as she lazily headed towards the bed, dropping her small black purse on the nightstand. She walked back towards him, boot over boot, slinky, sexy. Her eyes drilled into his, her chin slightly down, staring at him with desire. She knew all the tricks—no wonder her dance card was always full. She put her hands around his neck, leaned in and nibbled his ear.

"So how we going to do this?" she whispered into his ear.

"Nice and slow, but we'll have to wait a minute. I need my little blue friend to kick in." He held up a small blue pill. It was a breath mint.

"Too bad… I'm ready for you now. What do you want me to do while we wait?" she said, smirking at him.

"Take those boots off. And get on the bed."

She walked over and straddled the corner of the bed. She bent at the waist, exposing her ample cleavage to him, gripped the zipper of the left boot and slowly ran it to the heel. Then she lifted her leg straight in the air and pulled off the boot. *No underwear,* he thought. *Good. That was a real pain on the last one.* She repeated the act with the second boot, and then backed her way up the bed, leaning against the padded headboard.

"Now what? I'll do anything you ask."

"You do drugs?" he asked.

"Sometimes."

"Want to shoot up while we wait?"

"I really shouldn't. I'm trying to cut back."

"I have some really good stuff with me. Medical grade."

"Oh, okay. Why not," she said, smiling.

He walked over to her and took a small pouch from his jacket pocket. He set the pouch on the edge of the bed and unzipped the edge. He pulled the syringe from its holster, laying it next to the case. He pulled out a small vial of clear liquid.

"What is that stuff?" she asked, looking at the vial.

"Just wait, it's amazing."

"Cool," she said, holding out her left arm.

He ran his fingers through her brown hair, over her shoulder, and down her lightly tanned arm to her elbow. He could feel a frequently used vein with his thumb. He probably could do it without a tourniquet. He pulled a small piece of rubber from the case and wrapped it gently above the vein. He tied it off tight. The vein popped up prominently in the crux of her elbow. He tapped the syringe, squirted a small bit of the liquid out of the end and deftly inserted the needle into the vein. He pressed the plunger, releasing the liquid into her blood stream. *It won't be long now*, he thought, placing the syringe and vial back in the case.

"Wow, I didn't even feel that. You're really good with that needle."

"Well, thank you. Wait until you see what else I'm good with."

He lit a cigarette and sat on the end of the bed. He turned so he could see her. She was beautiful. He wished he could have her first, but it would never happen. Maybe a decade ago, but definitely not tonight. While he took long drags on his cigarette, he wondered if anyone understood what he was doing—saving lives, important lives.

"Wow, this is some good stuff," she said.

"I told you."

"I know. I'm worried I might fall asleep before we have our fun though."

"Oh, don't be worried. That is exactly when our real fun will begin," he said, pulling his scalpel from his jacket pocket, the fresh blade glimmering.

7.

Rogan still had enough friends in the department to warrant a little special treatment. Instead of general lockup, Rogan sat alone in a cell at the end of the hallway, well away from any other criminals. The long, lonely night did not dissuade his active mind. If anything, it gave him more time to think. Rogan started feeling that feeling again, the itch in his blood when he was all in on an investigation. The feeling of the hunt. All he had at this point were unanswered questions, but in his experience, questions always lead to answers. He had to follow the needle. He would need to find out what the needle contained and how it ended up at the Amdahl.

A key striking home down the hall pulled him out of his thoughts. He wondered if it could really be morning already. One step into the hall, and he knew exactly who approached. The footfall of her stiletto heels was as unmistakable as her peach-and-ginger-scented perfume.

Rogan closed his eyes and tried to guess what she would be wearing. Definitely a gray suit, probably the dusty gray one with the slightly ruffled collar, a red button-up shirt, and, of course, black stilettos with red bottoms. Rogan imagined her blonde ponytail bouncing off the nape of her neck as the steps grew closer. Rogan used to love watching her turn on one of her high heels and storm away, the ponytail swaying with every angry step. Even though her clenched fists were usually the result of something stupid that Rogan had said, he always smiled a little at himself as she stomped away. He had only seen her hair down a few times. Because of his own idiocy, he was sure that ship had long since sailed.

She came to a stop in front of Rogan's cell door. *Dark pink blouse today. So close*, thought Rogan. Her ice blue eyes took him in for a moment, and then she said, "Rogan why are you so damn stupid?"

"That is one of many unsolved mysteries. Nice to see you, Sam."

"Why do I feel like the only time I see you is when Coop is cleaning up one of your messes?" she asked.

"So you're saying you'd like to see me more?"

Sam just stared at Rogan, her tight pink lipsticked lips tensing by the second. "Seriously Rogan. If you don't knock it off, you are going to get yourself into some kind of trouble that Coop can't erase."

"Oh come on, Sam, I'm not so bad."

"Should we start with the multiple breaking and entry charges, or maybe the trespassing? Or how about defacing public property?"

"Those were all misunderstandings. Plus, the number of paranormal reports has been drastically reduced since I cut the head off of that statue. I should have gotten a medal."

"Always ghosts and games with you. I hear it's a demon this time?"

"Did you see the writing?"

"Rogan, I've known you for a long time, and I know for a fact you don't believe in demons. Don't you remember during that drug bust we staked out in Southtowne? You told me all about it."

"I remember sharing onion rings and a bottle of cheap wine from the gas station."

That almost managed to drag a smile out from Sam Stone's angry lips. Rogan swore he saw a subtle rise on the left side of her mouth. If she wasn't so mad at him, he was sure she would have smiled about the onion rings and wine. Those long stakeouts were the beginning of their short relationship. Rogan originally met Sam in the Police Academy. She was brilliant, and beautiful. Rogan lacked the mojo to even consider talking to her back then. Then, through some sort of divine intervention, the two were paired together in narcotics shortly after graduating.

"You're right, Sam. I was just trying to help out the sister of the deceased. She deserves to know what happened to her sister."

"Then let us handle it."

"A murdered call girl in the Basin? How long do you think the upper brass is going to let you keep that case open?"

"Even if you're right about that, you're a civilian, Rogan. You can't go poking your head around."

"Yeah, at least it was just disturbing a crime scene. Your buddy Rod wanted to book me for murder."

"I know you two have whatever it is you two have, but he was actually building a pretty strong case against you.

"Was? Surprised he stopped."

"Had to. You have a rock solid alibi for last night, since you were sitting right here at the police station."

"What happened last night?"

"Another girl murdered at the Amdahl. Looks like we might have a serial killer. Which is why, Rogan, I need you to stay away from this."

"Same building, same MO? Ballsy…"

"Rogan…"

"Heart gone again? Did they find a needle this time?"

"Seriously, knock it off, or I leave you in that cell."

"Fine, but at least tell this convict what the message said this time."

"The wicked sow wickedness. Now that is enough. Promise me you'll drop this? Let me do my job. You go back to pancakes and ghosts, okay?"

Rogan just nodded with his eyes cast downward at the dirty cement floor like a scolded child. He did not speak because Sam would know that he was lying. Sam turned the heavy key in the old prison door lock, making Rogan once again a free man.

"McKenzie is waiting for you in the lobby. I'll never understand why she puts up with you."

With that, Sam turned on her heel. Rogan stood in the doorway of the cell and watched as she strode away, heels clicking, the red from the bottom of her shoes flashing, and ponytail bouncing. Rogan smiled. *She still cares*, he thought as she disappeared through the door at the end of the hall.

Rogan saw McKenzie pacing between a fake ficus and a magazine stand when he entered the lobby. She stopped, looked at him, shook her head, and walked towards the entrance. Rogan followed. Neither of them said a word until they pulled away from the station in McKenzie's biofuel Volkswagen. The small blue car always smelled of French fries and burger grease. According to McKenzie, the smell was worth not going to a gas station, but it just made Rogan hungry. McKenzie was only an environmentalist by correlation. In actuality, she was just cheap—or frugal, as she liked to call it. Being "green" often saved money, and therefore McKenzie was on board with the movement.

As the blue Volkswagen rolled past the tall buildings of downtown, Rogan could feel the tension oozing from McKenzie. He could tell she was mad, and most likely she was mad at him. He was also certain that if he thought about it hard enough he could ascertain what he had done. Before he could come up with the root cause of the anger cloud floating around McKenzie, she broke the silence.

"Okay, obviously I'm mad at you. That was a dumb move, Rogan. What the hell were you thinking?"

"Well..."

"Can I finish?"

"But you asked me... Never mind. Go on."

"What if that wouldn't have been just a sedative in that needle?"

Rogan made to speak but was met with a finger between his eyes.

"That was rhetorical. You could have been killed. You shouldn't have gone there last night, and you definitely should not have gone alone. I'm just so mad you didn't call me. Then you put me in that position. I had to call Rod, of all people, because for all I knew you were dead laying on that nasty ass shag carpet."

"I'm sor.."

"Not done. I know you, Rogan. I've known you for a long time. I haven't seen you with that look on your face, since, well before all the bad happened. Sarah got that same look when she dug into a case. I always knew it meant she wasn't going to give up on it no matter what anyone said. So I know that no matter what Coop says, no matter what Sam says, no matter what I say, you aren't going to stop are you?"

"I..."

"Again, rhetorical, listen, would you? I've been chasing ghosts with you for four years, and I love it. I know you do, too, but I also know it isn't enough for you. You need the action, you need to put bad guys away. I get that. I've seen it on your face for months now. Whether you want to admit it or not, you are *miserable*, Rogan. You need this. I know that. So, if you promise to stop keeping me in the dark and let me help, and listen to me when I talk, I won't say another word and we can catch the creep that killed those girls together."

Rogan looked over at her, unsure if he should speak or not. He decided to risk it. "Thanks, Mac."

"Not what I wanted to hear."

"I'm sorry?"

"Warmer."

"I promise not to keep you in the dark."

"Ever again?

"I promise to not keep you, my dearest and closest friend, in the dark on anything ever again.

"Good boy."

Very few people could put Rogan in his place. McKenzie was one of them. He assumed her power came from his late sister. Sarah Rogan could always tell Rogan how it was and how it was going to be. Since McKenzie and Sarah spent an exorbitant amount of time together growing up, Rogan figured she must have gained some of Sarah's uncanny ability to shoot Richard Rogan down through osmosis.

It came as a surprise to Rogan that McKenzie was okay with him getting back into the crime game. He felt confident that she would side with team Cooper on the subject. McKenzie was as much Rogan's sister as Sarah had been. After Sarah died, the only person Rogan consulted before hanging up his police shield was McKenzie. After all the death she had seen, McKenzie was in full support of Richard giving up the life that took his family.

"I'm a little surprised you are okay with this," said Rogan.

"I was not okay with it yesterday or last night. But that girl that was killed last night, her name was Vickie, and she did not deserve to die like that."

"You knew her?"

"I was starting to. She went to my Drug Addicts Anonymous class—one of my best students. She was so nice, and you could tell she was going to make it, ya know? She was struggling with keeping clean, but she was making progress. I know she was a 'working girl,' but she talked about saving her money instead of snorting it. I really think she would have made it out of the Basin, Rogan. I really do. All she needed was a little more time. I was getting through to her. I know I could have helped her."

McKenzie hadn't given much thought to what she would do after high school until her mother overdosed the day of graduation. McKenzie enrolled in the local college and took psychology and sociology classes with the hopes of one day becoming a drug and alcohol counselor. After college, she began work with a local community outreach program. She specialized in helping the families of drug addicts cope with their situation. Given her home life growing up, she was uniquely qualified to help the families. She also led a number of classes for drug addicts to help them crawl their way out from under their addictions.

"I'm sorry, Mac," said Rogan.

"It's okay. I didn't know her that well. She had only come to a couple classes. I do want to find the freak cake that did this, though."

"We will, I promise," said Rogan, squeezing McKenzie's shoulder. "Let's get some pancakes, and then I need you to take me to the hospital."

"The hospital? Why, are you feeling okay?"

"I'm fine, but we need to follow our only lead. That damn needle that put me out."

Karin hadn't slept the night before. She felt that she had done the right thing, but her mind bounced back and forth along her personal scale of morality. Wherever that heart came from, it would have been wasted if she would have called it in. The heart had been out of a body for at least a couple hours, and its viability would have come and gone by the time they got the paperwork sorted out. She also felt relieved that Hope would be okay. On the other side of the scale, she knew she had done something wrong. Not only was accopting the heart legally wrong, but it was morally wrong as well. By accepting that heart, she was opening up a door to a dark world. The rules were in place for a reason. She hoped that what she did would not have any unintentional side effects.

After her morning coffee, she stopped by to see Hope. The small girl was asleep. Karin stood by her bedside for a few minutes, running her fingers through Hope's blonde strands of hair. She was a beautiful little girl that would now grow into a wonderful woman. Karin pulled out Hope's chart. She was taking to the heart perfectly. There were no signs of rejection. Karin made a note to remember to compliment Dr. Paige on a job well done. Karin finished her rounds and headed for her office to do some paperwork. She filled her coffee at the coffee kiosk in the lounge on the way, turned, and almost slammed into Winston.

"Oh, Winston, I'm sorry. I almost covered you in coffee."

"Well, I've been covered in worse, my dear. How are you today?"

"I'm doing well, Winston. How are you?"

"Very good. I heard through the grapevine that little Hope got a heart."

"Yes, she did. It was quite miraculous."

"I was so glad to hear it. If she got one, maybe my grand-daughter's time will be soon."

"I sincerely hope so, Winston. Jenny is a wonderful girl."

Winston nodded and walked off. Karin nodded to herself. She did the right thing yesterday. She couldn't tell anyone about it, but she still felt like she had made the right choice.

Karin walked to her office, opened the door, and stared at the red cooler sitting on her desk. She quickly closed and locked the door. *It could not possibly be another heart*, she thought as she stared at the cooler. Who is this new courier? Two mistakes in a row? She took a deep breath and opened the cooler. In the bottom sat a perfectly healthy-looking human heart. She closed the lid, glancing around her office like she was hiding a secret. She took the cooler to the receiving lab. The heart was viable, and a perfect match for another child under her care. She knew this was wrong. But, after all, she had done it yesterday. *What's one more?* After this one, she promised herself she would call in and see about the courier. Karin called Dr. Paige's office.

"Paige."

"Hi Jim, its Karin."

"Morning Karin, how are you?"

"I'm great. I stopped to see Hope earlier. She seems to be doing well."

"Oh yes, she's a little fighter. I still can't believe how perfectly that worked out. She goes into arrest and then minutes later a heart arrives. Makes you want to believe in a higher power."

"It does, indeed, and I have some more good news."

"Oh?"

"Yes it seems luck is with us, another healthy heart arrived today."

"You don't say," said Dr. Paige.

"Yep, prep for surgery. I'll walk it down."

Karin hung up the phone. She chewed on her lower lip and stared at the coolor. She knew this was wrong, but wouldn't it also be wrong to waste it? Maybe Dr. Paige was right, maybe some higher purpose was being served. Karin carefully transferred the organ to a white surgical cooler and carried it down to the surgical suite.

8.

After pancakes with blueberry syrup, Rogan and McKenzie drove to the hospital. Rogan figured there were few people that loved going to the hospital. He was no exception. All of his visits had been for bad reasons, either the death of someone he loved, or to interview someone who had something horrible happen to them.

Rogan and McKenzie walked down the halls of the hospital towards the wing Rogan had been a guest of the previous evening. As they walked by, Rogan glanced at the bed he had been handcuffed to. It was now occupied by a white-haired woman with her hands crossed gracefully over her chest.

The nurses' station served as the nerve center for the wing. It was a nexus of activity with pastel clad nurses rushing in and out, swapping charts and tools to care for the many people under their watch. Rogan saw his nurse from the night before in vibrant pink leaving the station and rapidly walking away down the hall. Rogan and McKenzie switched to a trot to catch her.

"Excuse me," said Rogan, fighting to keep his breath.

"Yes?" replied the nurse. She slowed but did not stop.

"I don't know if you remember me, but you took care of me yesterday, Richard Rogan?"

"Oh yes, of course, I thought you were...arrested," she said, eyeing Rogan.

"That was just a terrible misunderstanding. Wrong place, wrong time sort of thing."

"I see. Well are you here for a follow-up? If so, check in back at the registration desk, and someone will check you in."

"No. no, I'm fine. I was hoping to ask you a couple questions?"

"Okay, but I don't have much time."

"I don't need much, can we stop?" asked Rogan.

"No, you can walk with me though. No time to stop. Got paged," replied the nurse.

"Where are we headed?" asked McKenzie.

"Transplant. I am scrubbing in on my first heart transplant!" said the nurse, looking excited.

"Oh, well then, we won't waste any time! What was in that needle that stuck me?" asked Rogan.

"Hmm, I don't remember, let me look."

The speed walking nurse flipped on the tablet PC that had been swinging with her arm. Thanks to advances in medical information systems, every staff nurse had access to volumes of information about patients, drugs, and other clinical data right at their fingertips. Without slowing a step she tapped at the screen, easily dodging other staff members and patients as she went. Rogan stumbled over an IV pole and nearly took out a woman with a walker.

"Okay, here it is. Propopental."

"What is that?" asked McKenzie.

"A very strong sedative, surgical strength."

"Where would someone get it?" asked Rogan.

"Usually in the arm before major surgery," replied the nurse.

"Could a non-medical person get it from somewhere for non-surgical uses?" asked McKenzie.

"Absolutely not. It is a controlled substance."

"Where does the hospital get it from?" asked Rogan.

The nurse tapped on the screen again with her closely trimmed, unpainted fingernails. Her light almond eyes scanned the digital output of the screen. Then she shrugged and looked up at Rogan and McKenzie.

"We don't. According to this, that particular sedative is no longer used here. To bring someone to a long lucid state took a high dosage, which caused a ton of nausea during recovery, so the product was replaced with a newer alternative that has fewer side effects."

"Lucid state? Oh my God, do you think those girls could tell what was happing to them?" asked McKenzie.

"I can tell you I don't remember a second from being under, and that was a small dose."

"It does depend on the dosage used. Typically, with a drug like Propopental, the patient does not remember a thing."

"When the hospital discontinued the product, what would have been done with the remaining stock?" asked Rogan.

The nurse tapped on the screen again, sliding her finger a few times as the trio entered the transplant wing. "Usually it's disposed of or returned, but it looks like our stock was reassigned."

"What does that mean?" asked Rogan.

"We gave it to another hospital or clinic. Probably because in very small doses it can be used as a local anesthetic for minor surgeries and procedures."

"Any idea where it went?"

"Doesn't say, but the coordinating physician is always listed. Looks like it was Dr. Paige."

"Who is Dr. Paige?"

"Doctor here at the hospital. Kind of weird, but incredibly skilled," said the speedy nurse, finally coming to a stop in front of a set of large metal swinging doors.

"Well, this is my stop," she continued. "Hope I was of some help."

"You most definitely were. Thank you so much. Have fun in there," said Rogan.

"Oh, I will. This is going to be great! My first heart!"

"Nurses are so weird," said Rogan as the last shot of pink disappeared through the doorway.

Rogan and McKenzie managed to find out that Dr. Paige was in today, but that his schedule was full. The nice receptionist that Rogan somehow sweet talked told him that Dr. Paige always went to the physicians lounge for lunch. After tracking down the location of the lounge, which had a keycard door, Rogan and McKenzie found a place to sit at a coffee kiosk that provided a view of the door to the lounge. Rogan bought each of them a large cup of flavored coffee. They watched doctors come and go out of the room, waiting and sipping.

"Think this Paige guy had anything to do with this?" asked McKenzie.

"Not likely, but hopefully he can keep us on the path. We'll have to see how the talk goes. Angus get anything off the investigation? Any shots of that apparition?"

"No, we haven't gotten our stuff back from the cops yet."

"Did you see it?" asked Rogan.

"Maybe. I mean I thought I saw something by the window, and then next thing I knew you face planted and ran off."

Rogan had clearly seen the apparition by the window, and he saw it fly straight through him. He wondered why he was the only one that could see it. Mac was in the room when it happened, but she maybe only caught a glimpse. He hoped that they would find something in the video footage.

"So when you found the body, you said something about why did she lead me here. Who is she?" asked McKenzie.

"The ghost. I have this feeling that it's a she. I can't explain it."

"It's so weird that it led you straight to that room. It completely blows the idea of stored energy out of the water. No way was that just a coincidence," said McKenzie.

In the paranormal world, a prevailing theory is that ghosts are stored energy. Energy left behind from a tragic event or a person that died in a horrific way. The idea explained why sightings always seemed to occur in the same place. Often different observers with no knowledge of the other's findings would report activity occurring in the exact same way. A ghost walking down the same hallway, an image in a mirror staring in the same way, or certain repetitive noises, like footsteps were all examples of stored energy stuck in an endless and mindless loop. The theory suggested that ghosts had no sentient thoughts—they were not beings, just energy. What Rogan observed last night was not stored energy behavior. The ghost he encountered moved with purpose.

"I would have to agree. There is zero explanation for what I saw that night. I think I would catalog it as my first true sighting. I've been racking my brain for an explanation, but so far I do not have a way to debunk what I saw."

Rogan turned towards the door of the lounge and noticed a man matching the rough description of Dr. Paige he had gotten from his new receptionist friend. He watched the man slide his card in the door and disappear behind the set of carved oak doors.

"I think that was him." said Rogan. "Let's give him a couple minutes to settle in."

"And, smart guy, how do you propose we get past those big locked doors."

"I had assumed you already took care of that," said Rogan.

"You're so lucky to have me."

McKenzie had gone through a rough period in high school. She was still a hundred percent against drinking and drugs, but in her teenage years she opened her horizons to petty theft. It started off small, a candy bar here, a bottle of soda there. Eventually, it grew to wallets. McKenzie became an excellent pickpocket.

At the time, Rogan had noticed that McKenzie started to dress better. She always seemed to have money to head to the mall or the movies, which in the past were trips taken far and few between. His curiosity peaked; Rogan followed her to the mall one afternoon and watched as she lifted half a dozen wallets while walking down the hallway. She walked outside around the building to the dumpsters. Rogan watched as she took the cash out of the wallets and dropped them in the trash. Instead of confronting her, Rogan grabbed the wallets after she left and put them under her pillow at home with a note. The note said: *I know what you're doing. If you knock it off, I won't tell anyone.* Rogan didn't know if her pickpocketing career ended at that point, but he did notice that she was less flashy with her cash.

Rogan followed McKenzie over to the oak doors. She produced a physician's badge from her sleeve and slid it through the reader. The door oliokod. McKenzie smiled. They entered the large semi-circular room. The space was mostly empty except for a couple men in white coats chatting over a cup of coffee and a man sitting alone eating a sandwich by the floor to ceiling windows. The lone man taking notes on a small scratch pad was the man Rogan had pointed out. He had distinguished strands of pepper sprinkled in with his mostly salt gray hair. He had years on him, but he looked like he still stayed in shape. He sat chewing on the sandwich. With each bite, he would sit back for a moment and look out the window, and then he would go back to his scratch pad.

Rogan nonchalantly crossed the room, coming to a stop a few feet from the man's table. Rogan stalled his approach momentarily as the doctor turned towards them, his ice blue eyes staring over the rims of his silver-trimmed glasses.

"Excuse me sir, are you Dr. Paige?"

"Can't read a name tag? Patient? Family? What? And who let you in here?'

"None of the above. I'm a P.I."

Rogan hoped the doctor would not ask what it stood for. Dr. Paige sighed and went back to writing on the scratch pad.

"I don't have time for this today. Tell my ex-wife I am not hiding any money from her. If she wants to split something, tell her I want half her face and one of her breasts, because that's where all our money went."

Rogan and McKenzie looked at each other, unsure of what to do. The doctor, clearly annoyed, slammed his pen hand down on the open page and stared at them.

"Well? What are you waiting for? Get the hell out of here."

Rogan stood his ground, and McKenzie retreated a few steps. Rogan could only imagine what this guy's bedside manner was like. Besides his obvious anger issues, Rogan had never seen eyes so cold.

"Listen, I'm not here about your wife or any of her enhanced body parts. I'm here because two girls were slaughtered in the Basin, and you are my only lead."

"Working girls?" whispered Dr. Paige.

"Yes."

"Sit down, talk softly."

Rogan and McKenzie sat down cautiously, opposite the doctor, who was rapidly glancing around the room. He sat his pen gently down at a 45 degree angle on top of his notebook. Took one more look around and turned to focus on Rogan.

"I'm sorry. I'm always edgy after a procedure. Who was it? Monique? Candy?"

"Uhmm, no, it was a Vickie and a Tammy."

"Oh, well, I never saw them. I assumed I was in their appointment books. Who led you here? Dante, maybe?"

"No, actually, we are here because of Propopental. According to the hospital records, you coordinated a transfer of some of the sedative to another facility. We'd like to know where it went. We have reason to believe that it may have been used in the murders," said Rogan.

"Propopental. We donated it, I think. Can't remember exactly as that was some time ago."

"Do you have a record for it?" asked McKenzie.

"I should in my office. I would have kept a record of the hand off with a signature of who accepted the donation."

"Could we go get that document?" asked Rogan.

"Of course. I'm sorry I was cross earlier. It's just my ex-wife is killing me with litigation, and so far she has taken me to the cleaners. Those girls down there, though, they are good girls. None of them deserve to be killed. I'll help if I can."

Rogan and McKenzie followed Dr. Paige to his office. The small room had a thin slit window embedded in one wall. A solid oak desk sat in the middle of the room with the olive-colored visitor's chairs stationed in front and a large black office chair behind. Beyond the desk stood a book case that stretched from wall to wall and from floor to ceiling. The shelves were packed with medical journals and books on a variety of subjects. The desk itself was completely devoid of clutter. The only objects on the oak top were a yellow legal pad and an expensive-looking pen.

"I'm sorry, I never got your names," said the doctor as he walked towards a small bank of filing cabinets to the right of the oak desk.

"I'm Richard Rogan, and this is my assistant Mac."

"I'm Dr. James Paige."

"Can I call you Jimmy?" asked Rogan.

"Can I call you Richie?"

"Point taken. It's just that…"

"You wondered if I played guitar? Yeah, you're so original. I've never heard that one before… Sit down," said Dr. Paige.

Rogan scanned the book shelves while taking a seat in one of the olive chairs. Almost all of the books had medical titles or were from similar disciplines, like chemistry. On the lowest shelf, sandwiched between two large anatomy books, one title stood out. The book was half the height of the anatomy texts, and completely black, with small gold lettering down the spine. The words on the spine were written in Latin.

"Doctor, I don't mean to be snoopy, but what is that book?" asked Rogan, pointing to the black bound book.

"Oh. Yes. That is a book about demons and their study. Fascinating actually. Here's that document."

"Can I ask why you have a book about demons? Seems odd tucked in with all these science and medical texts."

The doctor dismissed the question with his hand and absently glanced out the small vertical window. "We had a troubled young man years ago that claimed he was possessed by a demon. I bought the book in the hopes of finding a way to reason with the young man."

In Rogan's experience, people who looked out the window while talking were distraught or lying, but he decided not to press the issue any further. Dr. Paige turned back to the desk and handed McKenzie the document he had found.

"So where did those sedatives go?" asked Rogan.

"Looks like they stayed right here in the city," said McKenzie. "Dr. Paige writes that he dropped one case of loaded syringes off at the free clinic down in the Basin."

McKenzie handed the document back to Dr. Paige, who filed it away again. As he pushed the heavy steel drawer closed, the pager on his belt began to ring and vibrate. Dr. Paige yanked the small black device off his belt and read the small screen. His eyes grew big, and he headed towards the door.

"Sorry, I have to go."

"No problem. Thank you for your help, doctor."

"Don't mention it. Good luck with the investigation. If you need anything else, just call," said Dr. Paige, rushing out of the room.

"Lots of coincidences," said McKenzie.

"Too many. Down on his luck doctor with anger issues and dead eyes, has access to the drugs, admits to being with prostitutes. He even has a book about demonology. Dr. Paige just became suspect numero uno."

"For sure."

"We need to check out that clinic and make sure they got all of those needles," said Rogan.

"Too bad it took us so long to track down Dr. Paige. I'm guessing they are closed up by now."

"You're right. The Basin night life will be in full gear by now. We'll check it out first thing in the morning.

9.

Cigarettes will kill you. *Seems funny now,* he thought, lighting another cigarette. He leaned against a wall a couple blocks down from the Amdahl. He wondered if anyone would be impressed by how he chose his targets. Before starting on the mission, he had followed each of the girls for a few days, getting familiar with their routines. She went and got her nails done around 6pm, and then stopped off at a little bar between 6-7pm. Now she was home. He thought about taking her there, but he didn't know if she had roommates. *Best to stick to the plan,* he thought. Two flawless plans executed so far. No reason to fix things if they are not broken.

He could see her silhouette through the window. She was changing, getting ready for work. She bent at the waist, making an upside down L, her long hair hanging. She took her hands and ran them through her hair, shaking loose the tangles. The street lights began flickering to life as she threw her hair back over her shoulders. He could make out the shadow of her breasts through the shade. She was petite, but her breasts were large. *Too large to be natural*, he thought. He wondered if that would pose a problem with extraction.

She disappeared for a moment, returning with a dress held up to her thin body. She held the garment, turning from left to right and back again. She stepped into the dress, wiggling her legs as she pulled it up onto her body. She took both hands and reached behind her, pulling a zipper from bottom to top. She leaned forward and grabbed her breasts, arranging them in the dress. She walked away from the window, and the light went out in the room.

He stayed in the shadows as she exited the front of the small apartment building. She was wearing a jade-colored dress. It looked amazing against her brown skin. She turned left, heading in the direction of the Amdahl. He followed her from across the street, staying a half block behind and holding tight to the shadows being cast by the old brick and stone buildings. He wanted to do it in the Amdahl again, but he knew that by now the police would be nosing around. Best to do this one somewhere else. He needed to throw them off the trail, if in fact they had even a hint of where the trail was by now. That is why he had to follow her. He knew that most of the girls would only take appointments at the hotel. He had another place in mind. One she would likely not go willingly.

He stood on the corner next to the Amdahl and watched as she walked into the abandoned store front across the street. *Going in to pay her pimp*, he thought. *Dante*. He had already decided that at some point he was going to kill him just for fun. One for the road, he'd call it. He wondered if that would be the line crosser. At this point he was killing to save lives, but he would be killing Dante just because he hated him. He knew Dante was into demons and all of that nonsense. That is why he put on the big show in the rooms. The messages and the gore. The whole thing made him sick, but he hoped that by planting enough evidence he could buy time by sending the police after this worthless pimp.

He watched her walk out of the door and head straight across the street. This is what he was concerned about, the way she walked with purpose. The jerk pimp had lined up a job for her. He would have to wait.

Twenty minutes later, she walked back out of the Amdahl. He could feel his heart racing. The hunt had begun. This was exciting. She turned in his direction and started walking. He ducked into the alley and watched her pass. She had on white, high heeled shoes to offset the jade of the dress. The dress was very short—one misstep was all it would take for someone to get a free show. It ran up and over her shoulder and looked Japanese. He could make out small bridges and bonsai trees on the dress as she walked under a nearby street lamp.

He had been watching her for a few days. He had come up with two possible plans based on her routine. Option one: she would not have a job lined up and would head down the row to try to hook a John. He would pull up in a car, rented for cash from a place that didn't care that he didn't want them to know his name, offer her a job, and they would head off. Option two: she had a job, at which point she would follow her normal routine and head to see her dealer. He would intercept her on the way. He walked out into the street after she passed and started following her, making sure he wasn't too close to be obvious. He stared at her rear as it rhythmically swayed left and right as she walked on her tall heels. Two blocks from the Amdahl she turned left. *She is definitely going to her dealer,* he thought. He ducked down a side street and picked up the pace. He would need to be in front of her before she got there.

He crouched behind the dumpster, waiting and listening. Each of the previous nights, she had walked down a short alley to cut a block off her walk. Tonight would be no different, except that now he was waiting for her. He would have to move fast. Even though she was small, he had watched her long enough to know that she had fire.

He continued to wait, wondering if he had made a mistake. Maybe she was heading somewhere else. Then he heard a faint clicking in the distance. He smiled. *Her heels*, he thought. He pulled a rag and bottle out of his jacket pocket. He carefully unscrewed the cap and dumped the bottle onto the rag. The clicking grew closer as he held the rag low and away, being sure not to smell it. His heart picked up pace again. His trap was about to be sprung.

He could see a long shadow jutting out past the dumpster. He leaned and cocked his head down. He saw her white shoes from under the dumpster, glistening in the dim light of the alley.

She stepped parallel to him, and he stood, his knees cracking. She stopped, turning around, looking in all directions. He froze against the brick wall in the thick shadows behind the dumpster. He watched her curly black hair turning about her head as she tried to find the noise. He held his breath, hoping he hadn't blown it. She laughed to herself, shook her head, and walked forward. He stepped out from the dumpster, coming up right behind her. He took one step and wrapped his left arm around her waist, pinning her arms to her side, pulling her in tight to his body. She felt good against him as she wriggled for freedom.

Before she could scream out, he brought around his right arm, holding the rag tightly over her nose and mouth. He was right about the fire. She fought with everything she had, but he had gotten the diethyl ether in her nostrils rapidly, quickly extinguishing her struggle. He felt her gestures weaken until finally she was limp in his arms.

He pulled her behind the dumpster and collapsed in a pile. Sweat ran down his brow, and his breathing was heavy and labored. If she had been any bigger or stronger, he wasn't sure he could have subdued her. He looked down at her lying across his lap with her eyes closed. *Such lovely lips*, he thought as he ran his hand through her black hair. He watched her sleep while he caught his breath. Then he stood up and opened a door next to the dumpster that led into a long-forgotten clothing store. He grabbed her under the armpits, clasping his hands across her chest.

"Definitely fake," he wheezed, pulling her across the threshold. "I suppose I'll find out for sure in a moment."

10.

The free clinic was located on the edge of what most residents considered the Basin. No one could say where the name came from, but everyone knew exactly what area of Queen City you were referring to when you mentioned the Basin. The area used to be downtown. During the town's early years, it served as the epicenter of commerce. As horses were replaced by horsepower, and the interstate system began stretching across the countryside, the city grew towards the interstates, leaving downtown all but abandoned. Years passed, and people forgot about the old downtown. The buildings ran down and most residents moved out to the more prosperous areas of the city.

A small group rallied to renew the downtown area. They petitioned to make it a historical district and to refurbish the old buildings. Their voices fell on deaf ears, though. The city had moved on, and the seedier elements took over, and the area eventually came to be known as the Basin.

The original builders of the city had built their main street at the bottom of a valley along the river, which, before the interstates, served as the main route of import and export. Some say the geographical location of the Basin at the bottom of a valley is the source of its name, while others claim that it is because crap, muck, and garbage always gather in the bottom of a basin. After the failed attempts to rejuvenate the area, the once-expensive studio apartments and classy store fronts were taken over by drug dealers and pimps. No one went down to the Basin unless they were looking for sex, drugs, or trouble, which could be found in spades on any corner or down any alley.

Rogan and McKenzie walked into the small waiting area of the Free Clinic. Rogan looked around at the many people waiting for medicinal care and saw one he thought might be a familiar face.

"Darla?" asked Rogan. "Is that you?"

"Mr. Rogan! Yeah, I don't look so good do I?" asked Darla.

She was right. A ring of dark, puffy black encircled her left eye, leaving nothing more than a small slit for her to see out of. Her thin lower lip was split, and her cheeks were covered with purple and black bruises.

"What the hell happened?" asked Rogan.

"Oh it's nothing. Who is she?" asked Darla, looking at McKenzie with her one good brown eye.

"Darla, this is my partner, Mac."

"I like your hair."

"Oh, uhmm…thanks," said McKenzie.

Darla rocked forward and back in her chair, with her hands clutching her arms. Rogan wondered if she ever let her arms just hang loose. She looked like she had been in one heck of a brawl. She also looked to be wearing the same clothes she had been wearing when she met with Rogan at the diner.

"This is more than nothing, Darla. Who did this?" asked Rogan.

"Well, it's my fault really. I was sad about my sister you know, and so I didn't do any work last night. I know better. Dante, Dante needs his money every morning, and I didn't have none, so he had to remind me of my job. "

"Oh my gosh. I'm sorry, Darla," said McKenzie, taking one of Darla's willowy hands.

"It's okay. He beat on me pretty good, but I've seen worse. I'll be fine."

"Who is this Dante?" asked Rogan, fire burning behind his green eyes.

"He protects us, sets things up, and we pay him part of our earnings."

"He's a pimp," said McKenzie.

"Yeah I guess. Any luck on my case, Mr. Rogan?" asked Darla, changing the subject.

"We're following some leads. Have you heard anything down here?"

Darla's brown eye darted around the room. "No one talks down here, but I'm starting to think Dante had something to do with it," Darla whispered.

"Why would you say that?"

"Well after he hit me, he said, 'Forget to work again, and I'll make sure you end up like your sister. Bitches don't pay, bitches die. Your sister never learned. You better.'"

"Sounds like we better talk with this charmer."

"Also I had forgot about it, but when he was slapping me with the back of his hand, I noticed he had a pentagram on his wrist before I blacked out. Isn't that a demon thing?"

"It can be. Dante doesn't sound like a pagan, so, probably. Where can we find him?"

"I've never been to his place. We always meet him at the old hardware store across the street from the Amdahl."

Before Rogan could inquire further, a heavyset nurse walked out from the back and called Darla's name. Darla tried to smile as best she could through her wounds as she stood up and went with the nurse.

"After this, we need to go find Dante," said Rogan. "I'll need you to talk me out of killing him when we get there."

After twenty minutes, the nurse emerged again and called Rogan's name. Rogan and McKenzie were led to a small exam room where they waited another twenty minutes for the doctor. With a knock on the door, an older man entered the room in a starched white lab coat. The coat was buttoned up, showing only a sliver of the green plaid shirt underneath. The coat dipped just below the man's knees, over a pair of dark khaki pants. He had crow's feet permanently embedded next to his eyes, and laugh lines prominently laid out from the corners of his mouth. He had a solid build, likely an athlete back in his heyday.

"Pregnancy test?" asked the doctor.

"What?"

"You're here for a test right? Find out if your soldiers broke through enemy lines, right young man?" chuckled the doctor, patting Rogan on the shoulder.

"Oh, no, no, that is definitely not it," clamored McKenzie.

"Sorry, that's what most young couples come down here for. What can I help with?"

"Well, actually, we are here about Propopental."

"The sedative? What for?"

"Well, Doctor…?" led Rogan.

"Everyone just calls me Doc, son."

"Ok Doc, did you receive a shipment of Propopental from the city hospital awhile back?"

"I don't rightly recall. We have some, but I'm not sure where it came from. You must be here about the robbery! It's about time," said Doc.

"Robbery?" asked McKenzie.

"Yes. About a week ago, some thugs broke in here and stole a bunch of medicine, including probably a half dozen doses of Propopental."

"Has anyone from the police started an investigation?" asked Rogan.

"No, you're the first."

"Okay, well do you have surveillance, or did they leave anything behind?"

"Our cameras stopped working years ago, though keep that between us okay? We keep them up as a deterrent."

"So what happened?"

"To the cameras?"

"No, with the robbery."

"Ahh, well I came in last Monday and found the back door kicked in."

"No alarm, I assume?" asked Rogan.

"No, never had one. The glass on the drug storage room was broken, and the cases were all smashed open. We lost a lot of medication, but the drugs were all that was missing."

"I'm sure you've cleaned up since then?"

"Yes, a new back door and all-metal storage room door. Oh, one thing. When we were cleaning up we found a belt buckle. One of the robbers must have dropped it."

"Do you still have it?"

"Sure, wait here," said Doc.

He walked out of the exam room. Rogan looked over at McKenzie, her feet swinging off the exam table. Her cheeks were flushed for some reason. A moment later, Doc walked back into the room and handed Rogan a small square buckle. The buckle was graphite colored with a beveled silver edge. There was a pentagram in the center of the buckle, which, when worn properly, would be upside down, indicative of devil worship. To each side of the full silver pentagram a capital letter 'D' was stamped into the metal.

"May we keep this?" asked Rogan.

"Sure, son, if it will help."

"One last thing, Doc. The girl that came in here just before us, Darla. Is she okay?"

"Oh poor Darla. I cannot even count the number of stitches I've put into that young lady's face. It's like that for a lot of them down here. Sometimes I feel like all I do all day is patch them up so they can go get beat on again. These pimps down here are getting more aggressive all the time. That one she's linked up with is one of the worst. I'm patching up his girls all the time. I keep hoping someone will put that scumbag in his place. Do you know her?"

"A little. We are also looking into her sister's murder."

"Oh I see. Was it Tina, or Tanya…Tammy I think. Lovely girl, a shame really. Well if you ask me, those damn pimps should be on the top of your suspect list. There's even rumors going around that they are beating on or even killing rival pimp's girls. It's getting worse and worse down here. We are busier every day. Speaking of which, I better get back, looks like there is a roomful out there yet."

"Yes of course, no problem. You wouldn't know where Darla went? She never came back through the waiting room."

"Same way I'll send you, out the back door. Usually when they are beat up like that, I send them out that way so they don't have to walk back through the swarm with their faces all bandaged and stitched."

McKenzie hopped off the table, and Doc led them down the hallway to the exit door. The clinic was small, two exam rooms, an office, and a couple of storage rooms. The building was clean and smelled of sterility, like most medical facilities do.

"Well, hope you can track down our lost supplies. We could really use them. Oh and if you two ever need that pregnancy test, come on back down. It'll be on the house. You two make such a cute couple," said Doc, holding open the door to the back alley. "Oh and one last thing," he said, holding the door with his foot. Doc reached into his coat pocket and pulled out with a roll of yellow smiley face stickers. "No one leaves here without a smile," he said sticking a smiley face on Rogan and McKenzie's jackets. McKenzie's cheeks were bright red and Rogan's eyes wide with shock as they walked out of the clinic.

"That was weird," said Rogan.

"Yeah, really weird. Our suspect pool just doubled," replied McKenzie, not making eye contact with Rogan.

"We better hunt down Mr. Double D, Dante."

11.

Karin felt like she was on top of the world as she walked away from the cafeteria counter holding a bagel in her mouth and balancing a cup of coffee in one hand and a bowl of cream cheese and jam in the other. She could not believe how lucky she had been lately. Two hearts show up unannounced—both of them are perfect matches for kids that desperately need hearts. She sat down by the window and looked out at the midmorning sun. She wondered if she would find another gift from the "heart fairy" when she returned to her office. She leaned back and sighed happily as she spread raspberry jam on one side of her bagel and cream cheese on the other. Then she put the two halves together and took a big bite. She scanned the busy cafeteria while she chewed. She could hear two young nurses having a conversation at the table behind her.

"Did you hear about the murders?"

"No?"

"Yeah down in the Basin. Three girls have been killed."

"So, not to sound jaded, but people are killed all the time down there."

"True, but get this. They found two at the Amdahl, and the other in the window of an old clothing store. But that's not the weird part, their rib cages were torn open, and their hearts were gone. How creepy is that…"

Karin gasped and dropped her mouthful of raspberry cream cheese bagel into her coffee. Her heart raced as she tried to catch her breath. Could the hearts she accepted be from murder victims? She had not allowed herself to think logically about the situation since she made the snap decision to transplant the first heart. Logically, she knew that those hearts would not be there if someone had not died. She never imagined that the hearts could have come from girls killed in the Basin. Could it be true? Could these hearts be theirs? She had received two hearts. If another girl was killed, would she find another cooler on her desk? If she did, what would she do?

Karin stood up and walked out of the cafeteria, heading for her office. Her hands were clutched at her sides, getting tighter with each short fast step. She stood outside her office door trying to calm down. Maybe it was a coincidence. Maybe.

She opened her door, swallowing hard as she looked at the small blue cooler sitting on her desk. She slammed her door closed, locking it. She made circles around her desk staring at the cooler. It looked like the others, though this one was slightly smaller and not medical. It was just a basic blue cooler. She leaned in, looking closely at the lid. There, on the outer edge of the lid, etched in, was the word Dante. She felt like she was wandering deeper into the circles of hell, so she found the name to be all too fitting.

She made several more laps around her desk trying to decide what to do. First things first, she had to confirm it was a heart. She pulled a pair of latex gloves from her pocket and put them on. Then she pulled down the cooler handle, gripping the sides of the lid. She closed her eyes and held her breath while she lifted the white lid off of the blue cooler. She waited a moment and then opened her eyes. There laying in the bottom of the cooler, expertly packed, was a human heart. She slammed the lid back on the cooler and latched the handle.

"Now what?" she said aloud.

She had two choices. She could transplant the heart, which she knew without looking would match one of her patients, or she would have to call the cops. She could maybe have talked herself into two hearts being a crazy coincidence. But not three, three was a pattern. Three was also the number of woman killed in the Basin, according to the gossiping nurses in the cafeteria. Knowing that after she made this call her career could be over, she picked up the handset and called the police.

Karin spent the time waiting for the police by chewing on her nails and continuing to circle the cooler. She couldn't take her eyes off of it. She dealt with death far too often, but this was different. These girls were deliberately killed, and their hearts were dropped off at the transplant center. A serial killer bringing in hearts for transplant. It made no sense to Karin. Not that the killing made any sense to her either.

Karin had thoroughly destroyed her manicure by the time the police arrived. A Latino-looking gentleman in a tweed coat knocked on the frame of the door to Karin's office, followed by a young blonde woman. Her hair was pulled back tightly in a ponytail. She was strikingly beautiful. *He isn't half bad either*, thought Karin as she waved the detectives in.

"Dr. Gilmore?" asked the man.

"Yes, but please call me Karin."

"Sure thing. I'm Detective Rodriguez, and this is Detective Stone."

"Sam," said Detective Stone.

"I understand you may have some information on the recent murders in Basin?" asked Detective Rodriguez.

"Yes. This cooler. There is a human heart in there. I understand that the girls are missing their hearts?"

"Yes, that is true. How do you know that this heart is related?" asked Sam.

"Well, it doesn't have any paperwork, and it is not in a medical cooler."

"May I?" asked Detective Rodriguez motioning toward the cooler.

"Certainly. I put on gloves when I handled it, so hopefully if there are any fingerprints..."

"Good thinking," said Rodriguez, pulling a pair of gloves from his jacket pocket.

Karin watched him put on the gloves. She liked his soft brown eyes and tightly cut hair. He was a handsome man. While Rodriguez examined the cooler, Karin explained how she found it sitting on her desk but that it should have been delivered to the receiving room. She also explained that she should have been informed that the organ would be arriving.

"As I'm sure you've heard, there have been three murders linked to this same case in the Basin. I don't suppose you have two more hearts lying around?" said Rodriguez, taking a seat on the edge of Karin's desk.

Karin had considered not telling them about the other two hearts, but she knew that they would figure it out eventually. She figured it would be better to come clean from the beginning.

"Well, no, not anymore."

"Excuse me?" asked Sam.

"This is the third heart that has shown up on my desk," said Karin.

"Where are the other two?" asked Rodriguez.

"They were transplanted into two of our patients," said Karin looking down at the floor.

"Why didn't you call in right away?" asked Sam.

"Well, I don't watch the news, and the girl that has that first heart...she was dying. In fact, she wouldn't have made it through the night. Then, lo and behold, a heart shows up on my desk. I was going to call it in, but she was going to die. I figured that whomever the heart had belonged to was already dead. Might as well do some good with it. I made a snap decision, and I'm sorry about that, but I'll be honest, I'm not sorry that my patient is okay now, and I'm not sorry that she'll be going home soon. Healthy for the first time in her life. I know it was wrong, but I'm doing the right thing now. You can take me away if that is what you need to do. I won't fight it," said Karin.

"Take you away? Karin, no we won't be taking you away," said Rodriguez.

What a nice man, thought Karin. She wished they were meeting under different circumstances. She didn't see a ring on his finger, and she had taken her ring off years ago, after her sham of a marriage fell apart. Detective Rodriguez picked up the cooler and turned it, examining all of the sides.

"Dante? Does that mean anything to you?" asked Rodriguez.

"Not beyond the Inferno of the same name."

"Sam?"

"No clue. I'll call it in—see if we have anything in the database."

Detective Stone stepped out into the hallway. Karin watched her leave and then turned her attention back to Detective Rodriguez. She thought he dressed more like a college professor than a Detective. She liked the idea that he carried handcuffs.

"So these other two hearts, when did they arrive?"

"One yesterday, one the day before."

"And when they came in, you just went down some list to have them…installed?"

"No, it doesn't work like that. Every person has certain genetic and biological markers. If the organ does not contain the same markers, then there is a high likelihood that the patient will reject the transplanted organ."

"Reject? Sounds like a night at the bar to me," said Rodriguez, smiling.

"Oh, I find that hard to believe, Detective," said Karin.

"Well, uhmm, what does reject mean in terms of a transplant?"

"Our bodies have extensive defensive mechanisms to protect us from disease and sickness. Obviously, they can be overcome, or we would never get sick, but our main defense is our immune system. In the event a foreign body, like a bacterium or a virus is found, our immune system goes to work to stop it. The same goes with a transplanted organ. If the body feels like it doesn't belong, it will tell the immune system to fire up and get rid of it."

"Is it rare that those two hearts matched?"

"Yes, actually, it is. The recipients of those hearts have rare markers. To have two hearts show up that almost match exactly to their unique makeup is, well, it's a miracle."

"These markers, I would assume you have them somewhere, on a list of some sort?"

"Yes, we do. When an organ comes in, we check it for viability and then compare the report with the list."

"Who would have access to this list?" asked Rodriguez.

"Me, a couple of my staff, doctors. Maybe a dozen people, tops."

"Can you make me a list of those people?"

"Sure, but you don't think one of them had something to do with this?"

"You said a heart never shows up out of the blue, and it is rare that it would match someone on your list so well. Makes me think that maybe these murders weren't so random. Maybe someone is trying to fill your list."

"That is crazy!" said Karin, slumping into her office chair. "None of my staff are killers. We all would love to save our difficult patients, but we all took an oath. Do no harm. No way. I can't believe it."

"All the same ma'am, I'll need that list."

Karin huffed and pulled a pen and paper from her top drawer. The detective started looking less attractive. How could he be so dense as to think someone in the medical field would have something to do with those grisly murders? He may dress like a college professor, but he had the intelligence of a beer-guzzling college dropout. She wrote the names, her fingertips turning red from the pressure she exerted on the pen tip. Once completed, she looked down at the list of colleagues and sighed. Maybe calling the police was a bad decision now that a witch hunt would ensue. She read each name and mentally crossed them off in her mind. None of them were killers. These were good people, the kind of people that worked long hours even though they didn't get paid overtime. The kind of people that save lives because they value life. Even Dr. Paige, with all his passion and eccentricities, would never think to take a life. She had watched him push beyond normal human levels of exhaustion during grueling surgeries. He never gave up, not until there was no option left but to record the date and time.

When she first called the police she was worried about herself and her career. She hoped that she didn't just open her colleagues up to scrutiny and possible damage to their own careers. She felt bad enough about what she did. If, by trying to do the right thing, she caused more damage than she already had, she would not be able to forgive herself. She folded the piece of yellow legal paper in half, placing her palm flat on top of it. Then she looked up at Detective Rodriguez. His cruel brown eyes stared back at her. What had she seen in him?

"I'll give you this list on one condition. I know you think I have to give you these names, but I don't."

"What is your condition?"

"These are good, honest people. Just because you feel the need to go on a wild goose chase doesn't give you the right to treat them like criminals. You don't possess the ability to count high enough to reach the number of lives these people have saved."

"I promise that they will be treated with the utmost respect."

Detective Rodriguez smiled down at her from his perch on the corner of her desk. *What a stupid jacket*, she thought as she flung the list across the desktop toward him. The door opened at the same time as he juggled the paper, trying to get a grip on it.

"Hey, we got a hit," said Detective Stone.

"On the cooler?" asked Detective Rodriguez.

"Yeah the name, Dante. He's a big time pimp down in the Basin. Bag it up, and let's go. Thank you for your time, Doctor."

"A pimp? Not a doctor, or a nurse? Imagine that," said Karin, glowering at Rodriguez.

Detective Stone looked back and forth from Karin to Rodriguez, raised her left eyebrow and walked out of the room. Detective Rodriguez stood up and pulled out a large clear bag from his jacket pocket. He opened it and slid the cooler inside.

"What's going to happen to the organ?" asked Karin.

"We'll need to keep it for evidence. It'll go over to the medical examiner."

"What a waste," sighed Karin.

"Well Karin, thank you for your time. Here's my card, if you think of anything else, or, you know, whatever," said Rodriguez, giving another fake-looking smile.

"Really? Wow, I totally get your statement about the bar now."

12.

Several hundred dollars and a volume of sketchy inform-ants later, Rogan and McKenzie found Dante's apartment. Dante's dwelling was located on the second floor of an aging four-plex, roughly six blocks from the clinic, and just a block from the Amdahl. Rogan and McKenzie walked cautiously up tho loudly groaning staircase, past graffiti-covered walls and broken bottles of all shapes and sizes. The hallway used to have natural hardwood floors, but now the floors were scratched, gouged and covered with a variety of paint stains.

Dante lived in apartment 2B. As they approached, Rogan noticed that the door was slightly ajar. With more than a little anger about the beating Darla had taken, Rogan stepped up to the door and kicked one big red Converse shoe outward, land-ing a solid shot next to the door handle. The door flew open, cracking off the interior wall and shakily returning. Rogan put out a hand to stop it and stepped confidently into the room, expecting to see a startled pimp. Instead, he stood staring at a dead pimp.

Rogan had seen more dead bodies than he cared to count, but McKenzie was still getting used to the idea. Rogan could have told her that you never really get used to it. She held her hand over her mouth and backed out into the hallway.

"I'll just wait for you out here," said McKenzie.

"Okay. I wonder what happened. That is a lot of blood, but it's not dried yet. Whoever did this might still be in the building." Rogan turned and looked pointedly at his partner.

"You're such a jerk," said McKenzie, stepping back into the room and closing the door.

Rogan smiled and stepped over to the body, making sure to avoid the blood splattered out and around the deceased. Rogan knelt down and looked over the body. He thought back to what his father had taught him. Get a cursory guess on cause of death and identity then start working the scene outside in. Using a pen from his pocket, Rogan lifted up a huge gold chain from the chest of the dead man. In gold letters accented with tiny diamonds, the chain's large pendant spelled out the man's identity: Dante. He was on his back, arms out to his side like the letter T. In his left hand he held a kitchen knife. A gash ran across his Adams apple, which seemed to be the source of the blood and the cause of death. Rogan carefully put the pendant back down and stepped away from the body.

"Rogan, check this out."

McKenzie stood in the living room pointing towards the far wall. On the wall, in red paint, was a large, upside-down pentagram. Under the pentagram sat a long low table with a row of different colored candles. To each side of the candles stood a skull, the one on the left was smaller, maybe from a goat, the skull on the right had curving horns, perhaps a ram.

"Red paint," said Rogan, thinking back to the original murder scene. "This guy was definitely into some bad mojo."

Rogan stepped back from the scene and tried to imagine what had happened. Did this guy really slice his own neck? The apartment was small, the kitchen and living room connected with a small hallway leading back to presumably a bedroom and bathroom. Rogan walked over to join McKenzie while his mind worked on the puzzle. Man alone, obviously cut across the neck. That kitchen blade couldn't be sharp enough to make that cut. The cut was clean, fluid. Something was not right with this murder scene.

"What in the hell are you two doing in here?"

Rogan spun around to the door to see a beautiful blonde and a worthless Hispanic man walk into the room. "Hi Sam, how are you doing?" asked Rogan.

"Rogan, why do I keep finding you at murder scenes?" asked Rodriguez.

"We just came by to talk to him. He was like that when we got here," said McKenzie.

"Shut it, Red, I wasn't talking to you."

"Rod, back it down," said Sam, "Rogan?"

"Yes, Ma'am. Mid-Thirties male found dead in his kitchen. Cut from ear to ear, bled out, no obvious signs of struggle, no sign of robbery, especially considering that god awful chain is still on his neck, only sign of foul play is the murder itself."

"That's not what I meant."

"He employed my client. She said that he threatened her, said he would make her end up just like her sister if she didn't play right. Also considering the giant pentagram, he is likely a Satanist. Could be our killer," said Rogan.

"*Our...killer?*" said Rodriguez. "I'm pretty damn sure you two were told to stay out of this. Over by the door, now.

Rogan and McKenzie moved to the entrance while Sam started walking the scene. Rodriguez called for a crime scene unit. Rogan leaned against the door frame and watched Sam work. He loved watching her work a scene, the intensity in her eyes, the meticulous nature of her movements. She knelt by the body for a moment and then began looking around the immediate area.

"Okay, CSU is on the way. What do you want to do with them?" said Rodriguez, motioning towards Rogan and McKenzie.

"Rogan, get McKenzie out of here before I decide you had something to do with this."

Rogan nodded, took McKenzie's hand and backed out of the room, leaving the door slightly ajar. He had McKenzie stand a few feet from the door against the wall, and then took several loud steps towards the stairs. He then turned and tip-toed back to stand next to McKenzie, motioning for her to be quiet.

"Well what do you think, Sam?" asked Rodriguez.

"Not sure yet. The body is still warm, though, so this did not happen that long ago. Also none of the blood is dry. Rogan was right, too, no sign of a struggle. It's like he just fell right here and started bleeding out," said Sam.

"Any chance it was…"

"No, Rod. Don't even go there. As much as you may hate the guy, even you know that Richard Rogan is not capable of doing something like this. If he can help it, he won't take a life."

"How are you so sure?" asked Rodriguez.

"Don't you remember how much time he spent on the range? Every morning, every night, he was down there firing off rounds. Know why?"

"No clue."

"I asked him once. He said that it wasn't enough to be good with a gun. He had to be great. That way, in the heat of the moment, he could take the right shot, not the easy one."

"What's that supposed to mean?"

"Rod, it's easy to shoot someone in the chest. It's hard to shoot them in the shoulder."

Rogan smiled. She was right, he respected life. Unless it was absolutely necessary, he never shot to kill. He learned the trait from his father, though his father did it for a different reason. Rogan's father said that to kill a man was to give them the easy way out. He shot to wound so that he could bring the guy in to face a jury of his peers. He wanted the guy to learn from what he had done. Richard understood that sentiment. He too preferred justice over execution, and certainly life over death.

"Woah, what's this?" asked Rodriguez.

"A note?" asked Sam. "What does it say?"

"I'm sorry for what I did, but their souls needed to be cleansed. I now go to my dark lord to receive my reward. Dante."

"Suicide?"

"Looks that way. Have to see what CSU has to say."

"Let's go," whispered Rogan. "I need to think."

Rogan and McKenzie sat side by side in Rogan's booth at The Diner. Rogan ate a stack of pancakes while McKenzie worked on a piece of strawberry pie a la mode. Rogan stared at the impression in the seat across from him, thinking about the case.

"Case closed?" asked McKenzie, a dabble of strawberry glaze hanging on the corner of her mouth.

"No, something wrong with that picture."

"How so? The guy was clearly a devil freak, and he copped to it in his parting note."

"True. But there is no way he slit his own throat with that knife. It looked pretty dull. That cut was clean, exact, and made by something extremely sharp."

Rogan continued staring at the seat across from him as he cycled through weapons that could cut like that. He also thought of Darla's face and the bruises she sustained. The knife was in Dante's left hand, but, based on the bruises, Dante was right hand dominant. There was no way that Dante's death was a suicide. Could his death be tied to the Amdahl murders, or was this just a convenient time for his competition to take him out and blame him for the murders?

"You ever going to let someone sit over there?" asked McKenzie.

"No."

"Rogan, it's been five years. At some point aren't you just torturing yourself?"

"It's his spot. He sat there almost every day of his life, and I've sat here. If he ever wants to come back and finish our conversation, I want to make sure his spot is open."

"You couldn't have known, Rogan. You have to stop beating yourself up every day."

"Scalpel."

"What? What does that have to do with anything?"

"We need to talk to Troll. Done with your pie?" asked Rogan standing up.

"Yeah, I'm done," said McKenzie as Rogan walked towards the door, "for now anyway."

13.

Rogan and McKenzie pulled up in front of the County Morgue. The building stood on its own with lush grounds surrounding the square two-story structure. The building was only a couple of years old; the city provided more than enough business to justify the expense of the massive facility. Rogan ran to the front door, held it open for McKenzie, and then half walked, half jogged through the long rectangular lobby to the reception desk. The receptionist looked up from her magazine at the excited Rogan.

"Hello, I need to speak with Travis Oleson please," said Rogan.

"I see, young man. Have a seat over there."

"It's very important. Official business, ma'am."

"Official you say. Do you have a badge to go with that sass?" asked the woman. She stared him down with her dark brown eyes.

"Just tell him its important, okay?" said Rogan, wind slipping from his sails.

"Oh I will, sweetie. Now take a seat," she said with the authority of a woman who had raised several children, all of whom were probably Rogan's age or older. Rogan and McKenzie retreated a few steps, turned, and headed towards the seating area.

"Actually," the receptionist called as they walked away, "you look familiar. Aren't you one of Travis's ghost friends? Yeah, I recognize the shoes. He has a picture of him with you two in front of some old creepy hospital."

"St. Ann's," said McKenzie.

"Creepy looking place, if you ask me. Don't know why you kids want to go messing around in a place like that."

"I'm sorry ma'am. Do you think it will be long?"

"You in a hurry, young man? Maybe some sort of ghost emergency?" said the receptionist, chuckling to herself.

"No, I just need his expertise."

"In ghosting or holding tools?" replied the receptionist.

Since paranormal investigation paid none of his bills, Travis maintained honest paying employment as a coroner's assistant while he worked on completing his medical degree. His job consisted of picking up dead bodies and handing tools to the medical examiner during autopsy, though sometimes he did get to run the X-ray machine.

"Cause, son, if its ghosting, I'm afraid Travis can't come out to play right now. He's in assisting the M.E. on a fresh one."

"A girl, from the Amdahl maybe?" asked Rogan.

"Wouldn't know, couldn't say."

"Fine. I didn't want to have to do this, since it's a private matter, but clearly you are not going to help us out here. Listen, I wanted to tell him myself, but please call back there and tell him his dad died," said Rogan.

"Oh honey, I didn't realize. I feel just terrible. I'll call him up right away, poor Travis. Boy like that needs his father."

Moments later, Troll's large visage emerged from the end of the long corridor that ran perpendicular to the long narrow lobby. Troll frantically waved one of his mammoth paws at Rogan, gesturing for them to meet him. Rogan and McKenzie walked towards Troll. They met two thirds of the way down the hall, Troll's girth matching Rogan and McKenzie's joined width. They followed Troll into a small conference room. Troll closed the door and stared at Rogan with wide gray eyes.

"What happened?" asked Troll.

"We need to know if the coroner found anything off the bodies from the Amdahl, other than that whole missing heart thing," said Rogan.

"What? What? You said my dad died."

"Yeah I couldn't think of any other way to get past Mrs. Brickwall back there in the lobby."

"But you said my dad died."

"Right."

"That is only for emergencies."

Rogan and Troll had settled on the emergency phrase years ago. It was meant to serve as a call to arms, meaning something had gone down that required Troll to drop everything and meet Rogan. The phrase worked because no one near Troll at the time the news was given would question him leaving immediately. It also worked because Troll did not have a father in the traditional sense. His mother, a progressive woman that had sworn off men, decided that when her maternal clock started ticking she would respond. But she didn't need a man to up and ruin her perfectly good life. So, she selected Troll's father out of a big catalog at the sperm bank. All Troll knew about his father was that his number was 1627, and that he was college-educated and loved racquetball.

"Troll, there is a serial killer out there, stealing hearts. We have to stop him," said Rogan.

"We do?"

"Yes, we do. Look Troll, this is very important to me. Can you please help out?"

"Here I thought you were going to tell me you thought a demon did it. You remember you're not a cop, right? I'm not supposed to tell you anything about an ongoing investigation."

"I wasn't on board at first either, Troll, but Rogan's right, we need to find this guy. You know the cops won't. A couple dead hookers in the Basin, who cares right?" said McKenzie.

Troll sighed and placed his large palms flat down on the table top, hanging his bald head. "Fine. What do you want to know?"

"Thanks, Troll. Were there any needle puncture marks?" asked Rogan.

"Yeah plenty. They were obvious drug users."

"Any fresh punctures though, maybe in an odd location?"

"They had fresh punctures, but like I said they were covered in track marks. The new punctures were in the same locations as the old."

"Signs of a struggle?"

"None."

"What about personal effects?"

"Normal stuff, condoms, some cash, hooker cards."

"They were registered?" asked Rogan.

Prostitution was a legal profession in Queen City. Someone could work in the flesh trade as long as they registered as a professional sexual service provider and were tested monthly for sexually transmitted diseases at an approved testing site.

"Yep, tested within the last couple weeks, too. Though one thing that was weird…the victims showed no signs of recent sexual activity."

"So the guy didn't sleep with them before killing them?" asked McKenzie.

"Or after," said Troll.

McKenzie visibly shuddered at the thought of post mortem activity. The information Troll provided swirled around in Rogan's mind. Each piece of information was a small jigsaw piece that Rogan's crime-solving mind was attempting to fit together.

"What about in the chest cavity. Anything off there?"

"No. The heart looks like it was basically ripped out. The arteries and veins were torn. Looked very violent, but kind of weird, too."

"How so?"

"The chest plate was sawed open with something incredibly sharp, and it was done with care."

"So?"

"Well, if he just wanted the heart, it would be much easier to just break a rib and yank it out."

"Maybe it was for the symbolism, the ribcage pulled back like that, like wings or something?" said McKenzie.

"Could be. Anything else odd?" asked Rogan.

"No, pretty standard after that."

"Any tranquilizers?"

"Inconclusive. There wasn't much blood left in the bodies to test. Which, now that I think about it, is weird too."

"Why is that?"

"Well, when he tore the heart out, blood would have sprayed everywhere because of the pressure release, but afterward it should have started to pool in the body cavity and the rest would have sat in the veins. There was hardly any blood left in the body."

"Think the freak train drained them?" asked McKenzie.

"Maybe, but according to the CSU people there was a lot of blood on the scene. All dried on the bed, the floors, splattered on the walls."

"You said the chest plate was cut by something sharp, a scalpel?"

"No, would have to be a saw of some kind."

"What about the skin above the plate?"

"Maybe, but it would be hard to know for sure."

"So we have a girl, cut open, heart torn out, no signs of a struggle. I say she was loaded up with tranquilizers, but the bad guy didn't want us to know so he made sure that the blood was unusable, but, according to what you found, blood should have stayed in the cavity. It should have pooled in the veins. Troll, are you absolutely sure that the heart was torn out?"

"Yeah, well, yeah I think so. We found one artery on the most recent victim that was not torn like the others. It looked cleaner, like maybe it was cut, and there was a mark on it."

"What kind of mark?"

"We don't know what it's from."

"Could it be a clamp? Could the guy have clamped off the veins and arteries, cut the heart out and then tore the veins out to cover it up?"

"Hmm…wait here," said Troll leaving the room.

While waiting for Troll to return, Rogan paced back and forth in the conference room, trying to put the pieces together. He was convinced that Dante was not the killer, but then who? Could it really be Dr. Paige? Maybe he was selling hearts on the black market or something. It seemed like he could use some cash to deal with his divorce. Or maybe he really was a Satanist, and he needed them for some ritual. Rogan's mobile phone began playing his long time ringtone, the theme to *Ghostbusters*, pulling him out of his trance.

"Rogan."

"Uhmm, hi, Richard Rogan, P.I.?"

"Yes, who is this?" replied Rogan.

"I'm Cinnamon. I'm Destiny, I mean, I'm Darla's roommate. She left your card on the counter. I didn't know who else to call."

"What is this about?"

"She's missing."

"Darla's missing?"

"Yeah, I haven't seen her since yesterday, and it's not like her to not come home. And with all the bad stuff happening lately, and her sister...I'm just real worried about her. Can you help?"

"Yes, we saw her earlier. Was she working the Amdahl?"

"No, after her sister, well...she refused to go by that place. Far as I know she was just going to look for some small jobs on account of her face being like that."

"Do you know where?"

"Usually stuff like that she just went out front of our place, but I never seen her."

"Okay, we'll look for her. If you hear anything, you call me back okay?"

"I will. Please find her, she's a good person. Don't deserve all this bad."

Rogan hung up the phone and slumped into one of the leather chairs in the conference room. McKenzie sat down next to him and put her hand on his shoulder. The two sat quietly for a moment, and then the conference room door opened and Troll strolled in.

"You okay?" asked Troll.

"Yeah fine, our client just went missing."

"We have clients?"

"Amazing right?" asked McKenzie.

"Don't even start. What did you find?" asked Rogan.

"I talked to the coroner, about the clamps. He said that would fit. He also has been looking at that artery under the microscope. He's convinced it was cut by a scalpel. Does that help?"

"It's got to be Paige."

"Motive, opportunity, tools and skills. Makes sense to me, Rogan," said McKenzie.

"Let's go get him and find Darla," Rogan stood up and walked out of the room. "Thanks Troll," he said turning back towards the lobby.

"Good luck man. Need me to come?"

"No, we'll be okay. Hey, and sorry about your dad," said Rogan.

Troll rolled his eyes and lumbered back down the hallway, while Rogan and McKenzie walked back to the lobby, past the receptionist and out of the building. The sun was setting over the tall building to the east of the morgue.

"Now what?"

"We find Dr. Paige."

Rogan flipped open his phone and dialed the hospital while he and McKenzie got into her car. After getting transferred several times, Rogan found out that Dr. Paige had called in sick.

Time was running out for Darla.

Rogan and McKenzie drove around the Basin, but it was a futile search. Unless they got incredibly lucky and Dr. Paige was out wandering the sidewalks they were just circling around looking for a needle that may not even be in the haystack. Rogan stared out the window scanning every alley and building entrance. He believed in luck, but without some assistance they would never be able to find Dr. Paige. Rogan held his phone in his hand, rolling it. He needed Sam.

"Just call her."

"I can't."

"Yes, you can. I know her number is still in your contacts."

"She won't help us. I've already promised her twice I would stay out of this. Three strikes, you know?"

"I know, but think about Darla, and the victim after that, and the victim after that. Rogan, we've got to do something."

He stared down at the phone. Mac was right. They did need to do something. They could drive around for days and never find Darla or Dr. Paige, and by then she would be dead and he might have killed a couple more woman.

Rogan couldn't remember the last time he had called Sam Stone. He'd kept her number in his phone, like the final link to her. Once he deleted the contact, his chances of fixing what had happened would be gone too. He thought of any other option—he even considered calling Rodriguez—but Mac was right, if anyone would help them it would be Sam. Even if she were mad at him, she would care. She would help because a life was in danger.

He pulled open his contact list and scrolled to S. There she was, Sam. A small thumbnail picture next to her phone number showed her kissing Rogan on the cheek while he held his arm out to take the photo. He remembered that day; they had gone to the county fair together. She loved carnival rides. They bought a load of tickets and rode every rickety ride at the fair. They took the picture on the tilt-a-whirl. Their backs were pressed into the half clam shaped car as the ride shot them out towards the edge. She laughed harder every time they whirled around. Rogan had tried not to revisit his funnel cake from earlier that day. As the ride slowed, he pulled out his phone and took the picture. He pressed call, next to the picture, and held the phone up to his ear. No answer, voicemail.

"No answer."

"What now?"

"I know where she is. I'll go talk to her. Why don't you head home, call Troll. See if he found anything else."

Reluctantly, McKenzie dropped Rogan off on the south edge of the Basin. He stood under the street lamp watching her go. He walked three blocks out of the Basin towards the river. There, on the river's edge, sat a small bar called The Wrangler. The building looked more like a cobbled-together shack than a bar. It was small, maybe two hundred square feet total.

Rogan walked up and opened the door, stepping inside onto the wooden floor made of treated two by tens. The floor creaked with every step he took. Along the south wall was a row of video lottery machines, eight in total, each machine in use. Opposite the video lottery row was the bar. It was a simple long table with wagon wheels sitting vertically against the front. Six stools sat in front of the bar, all of them were full. The six men all turned in unison to stare at the new arrival.

Rogan had dealt with this sort of attention for many years. Even though he was no longer a cop, he still gave off a cop vibe. Whenever he met someone of ill repute they always assumed he was a cop. Between the bar and the video lottery row were five small round tables. Each table could fit two patrons. Only one of the tables had an occupant. One of the small tables was nestled against the west wall, under the lone window in the building.

Rogan saw a familiar-looking ponytail sitting at the table. Sam sat with her back to the door, staring out the window overlooking the river. Whenever she had a hard case, or even a hard day, she came here. No one cared that she was a cop. No one even knew her. They all called her Blondie, and they all knew that she liked her whiskey straight up, and that was good enough for them.

Rogan walked up to the bar and ordered two double whiskeys. He asked the bartender to put some water in one of them. Rogan picked up the drinks and headed towards Sam, the floorboards protesting the entire way. He took a seat to her left and slid the neat whiskey in front of her.

"Tough day?" he asked, sitting down.

"What are you doing here?" asked Sam, still staring out the window.

"I need your help."

"Of course you do."

"You okay?" asked Rogan.

"Peachy. I have a serial killer cutting out woman's hearts, and my only decent lead bled out on his kitchen floor. Oh and this guy I used to date, who has hardly talked to me in five years, unless of course he got arrested for being a moron, suddenly shows up everywhere I am. Can't even drink whiskey and brood without him coming around."

Rogan watched her roll her empty glass in her hand, staring at the light glinting from the rim of the cheap glass. He had really screwed it up with her, probably beyond repair. She set the glass back down flat and slid it towards the window. The glass bumped off the sill, spun once and came to a silent stop. She sighed and reached for the drink Rogan had brought over.

"Well?" she asked.

"Well what?"

"What do you want? What can I bail you out of today?"

"It's not like that this time. It's not for me."

"Rogan, it's always for you. It always has been. Even when you do good things, it's for you. Some part of it is always for you. Just lay it out."

Rogan didn't want to argue. Sam took a long pull of the whiskey, still staring out the window. He needed her help, but she was right, he did not deserve it. All he could do was lay it out on the line and hope she would help in spite of him.

"Fine. Darla, the girl I am trying to help, she's missing."

"The sister of vic number one? Probably ran off or something."

"Sam, you know that's not true. Not with a serial killer on the loose. Plus, I think I know who took her, and who the killer is."

Sam raised her left eyebrow, with her whiskey glass poised on her red lips, she darted her eyes over to Rogan and slowly sat the glass down.

"How could you possibly know who the killer is?"

"I don't know if you remember, but I used to be a pretty good detective."

"I don't remember that. I remember a hot shot who thought he knew it all. I remember a guy who ran when things got too hard."

"Sam, I didn't come here to fight. Darla needs our help. I don't know anyone else that could help. Please?"

"Fine, but I am not going to stop taking jabs at you. You more than deserve it."

"Fair enough."

"Who do you think?" she asked.

"Dr. James Paige. He works at the hospital."

"Why?"

"Well, I have the how, but I'm still speculating on the why. I started thinking about him because of the syringe that stuck me. Turns out that stuff, Propopental, is outdated. The hospital doesn't use it anymore, so they donated it to a clinic. Dr. Paige oversaw the transfer of the sedative to the clinic. We went to talk to him about it, and found out he is going through a messy divorce, so maybe money is involved. He also had a book on demonology in his office, so he may have been into devil worship, which would fit the ritualistic killings. Or maybe he was trying to lead us off the path. I wasn't sure though, until we found Dante today."

"What did that dead pimp have to do with anything?" said Sam.

"What lead you there?" asked Rogan.

"Anonymous tip," said Sam.

Sam Stone was good at a number of things, but lying was not one of them. Rogan watched her nostrils flare as she said it, which was her tell. He wondered why she was lying, but he needed her help, so decided to look past it.

"Well, you don't actually believe that idiot slit his own throat with a kitchen knife do you?"

"No, I don't. The cut was too clean, and that knife was dull, and according to the medical examiner, the cut was made from left to right. The knife was in his left hand, which means he would have had to push the blade across his throat, which would have caused the knife to jump. What we saw was one long continuous cut, no way was it done with the left hand."

"Exactly, plus I am pretty sure that Dante was right handed."

"How do you know that?"

"He threw a beating down on Darla. The bruises were consistent with right-handed blows."

"You sure you didn't kill him? I remember how fired up you get when you see abuse."

"I'm not going to lie. The thought crossed my mind, but no. Anyway, that cut was made with a scalpel. According to the coroner..."

"You talked to the M.E.?" asked Sam.

"Say what now?"

"Oh that's right, Travis works there, doesn't he?"

"Maybe, I think so. I don't remember for sure. Anyway, it turns out that the arteries were cut, not torn. The cuts were consistent with scalpel cuts. Dr. Paige is a surgeon, access to the needles, access to the murder weapon, maybe selling the hearts on the black market or something. I think the tearing, and the messages, which were written in paint, not blood, by the way, were all smoke screens to lead us in the wrong direction. Darla's roommate is the one that told me she was missing. After she called, I called the hospital. Guess who called in sick today."

Rogan could see Sam rolling the clues through her mind as she sipped on her whiskey. He could also tell that she knew a lot more than she was letting on. It did seem inconceivable that she wouldn't have had some sort of lead on the case, even with Rodriguez bumbling around. He watched and waited. He had seen her work a case in her mind many times before, and he knew that soon there would be a moment of clarity, at which point her eyes would get big and she would smile as the puzzle pieces dropped into place. The moment happened five seconds later.

"I buy it. I think it's at least worth looking into," said Sam.

"You don't just buy it. You know it's money in the bank. Come on, Sam, it all fits. More important though, Darla's in danger. We need to find Paige. Which is why I came to you. Will you help me find him?"

"One condition," said Sam.

"Name it."

"Once we walk out of this bar, you never, ever step foot in it again. I can't have you ruining my little sanctuary. Deal?"

"You drive a hard bargain," said Rogan, looking around the bar. "I'm going to miss the service and the smiles."

14.

It would be a Merlot night, thought Karin. *What a roller-coaster of a day.* First she was happy because two of her patients were on the road to recovery, then devastated when she put it together that the hearts were from murder victims. Then she decided to call the police, and one of the detectives was easy on the eyes, only to turn out to be a complete jerk. Plus the heart was wasted. She still did not know what would happen with her job. She assumed that once the board found out what happened she would be asked to leave.

Karin lived in a developing neighborhood on the expanding east side of the city. She drove past big box stores and chain restaurants until the lights of the city sparkled in her rearview mirror. Another couple miles down the road she turned into her development. The neighborhood was built on a low, elevated bluff overlooking the river.

Karin's house nestled itself amongst tall pine trees, and her backyard was cut back to give her a full view of the river valley. She loved that she could not see her neighbors. The large old trees made it impossible to see from one lot to the next, and rules within the covenant of the neighborhood meant that the trees would not be taken down. Her home was her quiet oasis, away from the crazy city, the crazy schedule, and the mental and emotional strains of the hospital.

She pulled into her garage, parking her single car in the center of her three-car garage. She lived in a four bedroom home. Two of the bedrooms, including the master suite, were on the top floor, while two smaller bedrooms were in the walk-out basement. Karin walked into her large closest, hastily throwing her clothes on the floor as she pulled out a set of freshly-laundered, blue fleece pajamas. She loved the feel of fleece, especially when it was recently washed.

Karin walked down the long stairway into her basement, turned down the short hallway, and entered the end bedroom, which she had converted into a wine cellar. She ran her hand along the backs of the bottles, all pointing cork down into their individual holders. Karin came to the section of reds along the back wall of the room. She picked up and turned several bottles of Merlot in her hands, carefully reading each label, trying to decide on just the right Merlot to save her evening. After examining six bottles, she chose candidate number four, a twelve-year-old, full-bodied vintage. Karin walked out of the wine room, carefully sealing the door behind her. With the bottle of wine in the crux of her arm like a baby, she walked towards the stairs. One step up, she paused. She felt a draft on her bare feet. She looked around the dimly-lit basement and noticed that the patio door was ajar.

"Stupid," she said aloud, sighing to herself.

Karin walked over to the open door and stared off over the bluff as lightning cracked between sets of dark clouds. Then she pulled the sliding door shut and latched it. Some days she had her first cup of coffee standing out in her backyard. She must have forgotten to close the door. Living away from the city, she often forgot about security. Locking her doors and windows seemed unnecessary. One time she had gone on vacation for a week and came back to find she had left her garage door open and the interior door to her house unlocked. She did not find a single thing in the garage or the home disturbed.

One of her favorite features of her little oasis was the isolation. She could see no one from her house, and no one could see her house. She had the driveway purposely curved when the home was built, so that her house could not be seen from the road. Karin lived alone. People asked her from time to time if it was lonely, but she relished her solitude. At work, where she spent most of her time anyway, she was constantly surrounded by people. Out here, she felt completely alone and loved it.

Several years ago she'd gotten a cat, at her mother's insistence that it wasn't natural for someone to be alone. It lasted two days. She couldn't stand the thought of some little creature roaming around her home.

Karin brought her wine into the kitchen and popped the cork. Working up her best attempt at a smile, she poured a large glass. She swirled the wine around the oversized wine glass, letting the smell of the wine fill the air. She closed her eyes and took a long, slow sip, completely unaware that tonight, she was not alone.

* * *

Two glasses of Merlot later, Karin felt wonderful. All of her worries melted away as the wine in the bottle was replaced by empty space. It was not unusual for Karin to finish off a bottle of wine in a day, especially on a day like today. She sat reading a romance novel in her living room, sitting in her favorite corner chair with her overhead reading light illuminating the space.

Thunder boomed outside, lightly shaking the glass panes in Karin's living room. She sighed, looking out the window at the storm outside. It wasn't raining yet, but the constant booms were making it hard for Karin to get lost in the romance of her novel. She closed her book and decided to treat herself further. She walked into the kitchen and headed to the refrigerator. She opened the door and pulled out a small bar of organic dark chocolate. Karin liked chocolate almost as much as she liked wine, but the two together she reserved for particularly bad days. She unwrapped the bar and placed it on a small wooden tray. On her way through the living room, she grabbed her wine bottle and glass, placing them on the tray alongside the chocolate.

Karin walked into her master suite, past her walk in closet, and into her large bathroom. She sat the tray next to the triangular whirlpool tub on a small stand and turned the brass knobs to start warm water flowing into the tub. She walked back to her closet, slinked out of her pajamas, carefully folded them and placed them back on the shelf. She pulled her warm, fluffy purple robe off its hook and wrapped it around her naked body.

Still wearing the robe, she sat on the edge of the tub, letting her feet dangle in the hot water. She sipped wine, ate chocolate, and waited for the tub to fill up past the air jets. While she waited, she reached over to a small glass shelf built into the wall behind the tub. It contained several bottles of scented bubble bath and bath salts. She selected a lavender bubble bath with a chamomile salt. She took the long stick lighter off the shelf and lit the six large candles that sat along the ledge of the tub. Smiling, she swung her legs out of the tub and turned off the artificial lights, leaving only calming dancing candlelight. She let her robe fall off the back of her arms and onto the floor at the edge of the tub. She eased her way in slowly, pausing occasionally to acclimate to the water. Karin lay back against the tub wall, playfully kicking her legs in the bubbles. She drank some more wine and finished off her chocolate.

Karin had a hidden secret. She believed in psychics. In fact, she often called a psychic hotline when she felt like talking. With the wine coursing its way through her body, she felt like talking. With a soapy hand, she reached up and grabbed the handset off of the wall. She used to use her mobile phone, but she had dropped one too many in the tub, and it got expensive to replace them. Talking to psychics apparently made her clumsy. She held the speaker up to her ear but did not hear a dial tone. She hit the button on the phone several times, but still no tone.

Karin sighed. *No psychic reading tonight*, she thought. *Stupid storm…figures.* Karin dunked herself under the bubbles, unaware that at that moment someone was watching her.

✳ ✳ ✳

He ran through a checklist in his head while he stood watching her from the closet. Phone lines, check. Power, check. Doors locked, check. Car disabled, check. Battery out of mobile phone, check. He watched Karin relaxing in her triangular tub. She seemed awfully happy for someone who had rejected a perfectly good heart today. Someone who had let a girl die for nothing.

He had never thought of Karin as an attractive woman, though it turned out that the white lab coat hid a nice set of curves. One advantage he had gained by following his targets was a familiarity with darkness. He could see well in low light. Everything was still fuzzy, but he could see. He watched her running a loofa sponge up and down each of her arms and from her hips to her heels. He could see the bubbles making small trails down her smooth legs. Karin set the loofa aside and laid back against the rim of the tub. He waited and watched.

Ten minutes later, he could hear her breathing heavily. He slowly walked into the bathroom, pausing every few short steps to confirm that she still sounded asleep. He crept to the edge of the tub, and looked down at her. He wished two things in that moment, one, that she hadn't used so many bubbles, and two, that his soldier could still stand at attention. It was a cruel trick of nature. He still had all the feelings and all of the impulses, but he couldn't do a darn thing about them.

He licked his fingers and extinguished each of the candles, plunging the room into complete darkness. He closed his eyes and counted to ten. When he opened his eyes, he could see shapes and edges through the darkness. He took his hands and placed them just out of reach of Karin's head. A crooked smile formed on his thin lips. He quickly grasped Karin's shoulders and plunged her under the water.

Karin gasped for air as she broke the surface of the water. She quickly wiped the bubbles from her face, her head darting from side to side looking around the room. She put her hand to her chest in an attempt to slow her breathing. She sighed out one slow breath to calm herself. *Too much wine*, she thought, leaning back against the tub wall. The candles must have gone out when she splashed under. This was not the first time she had fallen asleep in the tub after almost a full bottle of wine. This time felt different, though. She could have sworn she felt hands on her shoulders pushing her under the water.

"Is anyone there?" she asked.

She waited for a response. Nothing. She sat as still as she could, held her breath, and listened. She could not hear anything. She took the back of her left hand and ran it back and forth across her nostrils, trying to get the bubbles out of her nose.

"I have got to stop watching those stupid ghost shows," she whispered.

Karin pulled the drain lever on the tub. She sat upright in the tub, letting her head fall forward. She rolled her head from side to side, stretching her neck as the water whooshed down the drain. Soon she heard the drain's final gurgle. All that was left in the tub was Karin and a mountain of bubbles. She stood up, reaching for her towel in the darkness.

She couldn't see a thing. She regretted not having a second light switch installed closer to the tub. She took a step onto the bath mat next to the tub and toweled off the bubbles, then wrapped her robe around her. She gingerly stepped across the cold tile floor to the light switch. She flicked the switch up, then down, then up, and then down again. The lights did not turn on. Karin sighed.

She walked out of the bathroom, past her closet, and out into the living room. She tried several more lights, but none of them worked. At least out in the living room area she could see a little. The moonlight cast beams of light across her white carpets. She walked to the island that separated her living room from the kitchen and picked up her mobile phone. It was dead, too.

"Great!" she yelled.

A crash of lightning thundered outside, the light flaring through the living room windows. Karin gasped and spun around towards her master suite. Out of the corner of her eye she thought she saw something move. She swallowed, hard, backing away from the door to her bedroom area.

"I have a gun," she lied.

Maybe she was seeing things. All the wine could be getting to her. No one would be in her house, right? She kept her eyes on the door and backed down the hallway. *Better safe than dead*, she thought as she grabbed her car keys off of the hanger by the door to the garage.

She opened the door, ran out into the dark garage, opened her car door, and got inside. Her hands trembling, she tried to put the key in the ignition. She dropped the keys on the floor. She felt around on the floor for them and turned her head towards the open door leading back to her house. She held back a scream as she watched a black shadow break one of the moonbeams in the living room. She picked up the keys off of the floor mat, fumbled around the ignition a few more times, and then finally struck them home. She turned the key, but the car did not respond.

"Come on, come on…," she said turning the key again.

Click. Click. Click.

"No…" she gasped.

She looked back towards the open door again. She could not see the shadow. She decided that tonight would be the first time she would meet her neighbors, wearing just a bath-robe. She got out of the car and ran to the back door of the garage. She turned the handle, but it was locked. She fumbled with the lock mechanism, finally getting the door open. As she threw open the door, she could see the dark figure of a man standing in the doorway.

Karin ran out into the moonlight of her backyard. Lighting flashed overheard. Barefoot, she took off towards the front of the house. She made for the woods that led to the next house over. She had never met the people living there, but she thought it was a younger couple.

Halfway across the grass lawn, Karin tripped over a small yellow lawn sprinkler, and sprawled flat out against the ground. She felt someone on top of her, holding her face into the ground. She tried to scream, but her mouth was full of grass. She could not move. She felt something jab into the back of her neck, and then a small amount of liquid diffuse un-der her skin. Then, everything went black.

He had not expected her to run that quickly. He had disa-bled the car as a precaution, but he had figured she would stay in the house longer than she did. He would have to give her more credit from now on. She was a fighter. His back still ached from maneuvering last night's girl into the old store front.

"I'm getting too old for this," he whispered as he dragged Karin's limp body back towards the house.

With her head pounding, Karin thought for a moment that maybe it had all been a dream. She knew she was lying in bed. Maybe she had passed out after downing a bottle of Merlot. It would not have been the first time, though usually her Merlot dreams were of muscled gentleman riding white horses, not of shadowy men pinning her face down in her lawn.

Her eyes hurt. She moved her arm to rub them, but she couldn't move. Something was holding her arm back. She tried the other arm, same thing. Her legs too, were restrained. She looked around in the dim light. She was naked. Her arms and legs stretched towards each of the corner posts of her bed, a loop of rope tying each limb down. In the corner of the room, she could see a tiny red dot, going from bright orange back to dull red. In the small amount of light provided by the moon, she could see wafts of smoke.

"Oh good, you're awake. I was starting to think I had given you too much."

"Who are you? What do you want?"

"I only want to deliver a message."

"What? What message? Untie me!"

"I will. You are very beautiful, Karin. Did you know that?"

"What are you going to do to me?" Karin began to cry.

"It's more about what I could do to you, Karin. Look at how easily I came into your home. I've been here all night. I saw you pick out your wine, I watched you get your bath ready. I want you to understand that I could do that anytime I want. I can always get to you, do you understand?"

"Yes. Please, please just untie me."

"I could have killed you tonight. I could have drowned you, could have made it look like an accident. Or maybe now that I have you tied up, I could have my way with you. What do you think of that?"

"No, please, don't. Why are you doing this?"

"Because you threw away my gift today."

"What? What are you talking about?"

"The heart, Karin. You let a perfectly good heart go to waste."

"Oh my God…"

"Yes, that's right. I'm the one that has been delivering you those hearts. I don't like that you wasted one. That means I killed someone for no reason."

"What do you want?"

"I want you to understand that if you do that again, if you waste another gift, I will come back here, tie you up, do whatever I want to you, and then cut you open like the others."

"But those women, you're killing them."

"They are nothing. Wasted life. Your life is valuable though, Karin. I would hate to have to end it. A heart will arrive tomorrow. If you do not have it transplanted, I will be back. Oh, and one more thing. I also put an insurance policy in place, just in case you aren't willing to do the right thing to save your own life. You have a patient, Jenny."

"Yes…"

"I have taken her."

"What! No, she shouldn't be moved. She's very sick."

"I know. She needs a heart—which I will get for her, Karin. Unless you do not accept my gift tomorrow—then I will just kill her."

The man took a long drag on his cigarette. Karin struggled against her bonds, trying to break free. The man stood up and walked around the bed. He ran his fingertips up her leg, across her stomach, over her breasts, and up her cheek. She shivered against his touch. He stood over her, and then breathed smoke down onto her face. Karin reflexively snapped her eyes closed.

She could feel his hot breath on her neck as he whispered into her ear, "I will kill her Karin, then I'll kill you. Do as I say."

She felt something stab into her neck and the injection of fluid. Then, once more, she slipped away.

15.

Sam watched Rogan walk out of The Wrangler, tipping his nonexistent hat at the bartender on the way out. She slammed the rest of her whiskey, picked up the three empty glasses, and placed them on the end of the bar.

"Thanks, Eddie. See ya," she said to the bartender.

"Anytime, Blondie. You need us to take care of that guy?"

"No, I can more than handle him."

Eddie nodded. Sam put her hands into the pockets of her navy pinstriped suit and walked out of the bar. Rogan stood next to her black, unmarked police vehicle. She opened the doors and slid behind the wheel. Rogan hopped inside, looking eager.

"I'm really going to miss that place. Well, more the people. So nice," said Rogan.

"How does it feel to be in the front seat of a cruiser for once?" asked Sam.

"Nice, actually. A lot more leg room up here."

Sitting next to Rogan in a police cruiser felt like a jump back to a time long forgotten, back to when she and Rogan were partners. They used to be quite a pair. She knew that if they could have made it a little longer they would have passed the arrest record still held by Rogan's grandfather, but it wasn't to be.

She felt bad about lying to Rogan. She also knew that he probably knew she was lying. He had a knack for reading people. Once he mentioned the scalpel, the needles, it all came into place for her, though he was wrong on the motive.

Sam knew the real motive. This Dr. Paige, in his own twisted way, thought he was saving his patients by killing to get them hearts. It all lined up with what they had learned from that doctor, Karin, at the hospital. She also knew that there had been one heart a day. If Darla was taken by Dr. Paige, it would be very likely that Darla would be the next victim. Yesterday, Sam would have driven straight down to the Amdahl hotel and gone room to room looking for them. The killer had changed his M.O., though, by killing his last victim in an abandoned store front. They could literally be anywhere.

"Thoughts on where we should start?" Sam asked.

"Well, let's confirm he's unaccounted for. Can you call in and get his home address?"

"Call in? Oh, Rogan, you've been out of the game awhile."

Sam swung the small video screen mounted in the center counsel towards her. She logged into the system and pulled up the people search app. She typed in James Paige. There were two results, one located on the east side, one located in north town. She drilled down into the results and found that the east side James Paige owned a clothing store. The north re-sult showed MD listed as his profession.

"Got it, upper north side."

"Wow that's fancy. Can you order take out with that thing? Orange chicken maybe?"

"Really...?"

"It would be handy for stake outs."

Sam shook her head as she pulled out of the gravel parking lot of The Wrangler. Before Rogan sauntered in, she had in-tended on drinking until she was well past the legal driving lim-it, stumbling to her car, and passing out in the backseat. It was a practice she had taken up over the years. Somehow, when she woke up, she felt a sense of clarity...and the need to vom-it. Most times, though, her morning-after hangover was ac-companied by a new lead, which generally made the queasi-ness worthwhile.

They drove on through the old neighborhoods along the river until they came to Dr. Paige's neighborhood. It was a gated community. A security guard sat in a small glass cubi-cle, clearly sleeping. Sam pulled the car up to the swinging arm blocking their path into the quiet neighborhood. She glanced over at Rogan, who shrugged back at her. Sam pulled her badge out of her inner jacket pocket and rapped it on the glass of the cubicle. The man inside stood bolt upright, turned, looked at the badge, and slid open the small window built into the wall.

"Uhmm, hey, how can I help you, officer?"

"We need to get in there," said Sam.

"Where you headed?"

"Can't say. Part of a very important investigation."

"Then I'm sorry, ma'am, but I can't let you in. I have to record all visitors and call ahead to get permission to open the gate."

"You noticed the badge, right?"

"I sure did, but it makes no difference. Those are the rules we have to follow. Unless you have a warrant."

"What was your name?"

"Stan."

"Tell you what, Stan. If you overlook the rulebook this one time, I'll overlook the fact that you were sleeping, and that I could have just let myself in. How about that?"

"Sounds fair."

Stan sheepishly closed the window and sat down. A second later, the orange-and-white-striped arm moved from horizontal to vertical. Sam eased on the accelerator and drove into the gated neighborhood. The neighborhood turned out to be a series of intersecting curved roads, designed to maximize the lot size. The roads were not clearly marked. Sam and Rogan made at least six wrong turns before locating Dr. Paige's home. Sam cautiously pulled the black car into the driveway. There were no visible lights on in the home.

"Looks like no one's home," said Rogan.

"Let's check it out. Maybe he's just sleeping or something. Supposed to be sick, right?"

Rogan and Sam walked up to the front door. Rogan leaned over the black metal railing trying to peer into the windows. Sam rang the doorbell and pounded on the door.

"Dr. Paige, this is the police. Please open up."

No answer. Rogan moved to the other side of the entry porch, craning his neck towards the large bay window. Sam rang the bell again and knocked louder.

"Dr. Paige, please open up."

Still no answer. Sam sighed, glancing around the property. The lots of the neighborhood were laid out in odd angles, which at this moment worked to their advantage. Not a single window from a neighboring home looked directly towards the property. She looked across the street—the houses were all dark. She placed a hand on the doorknob and reached into her jacket pocket for her lock pick tools. She turned the knob first, and much to her surprise, it was not locked.

"Okay, quick sweep. Be careful, don't touch anything."

"Got it. I'll work towards the garage, check for cars."

Sam nodded. Rogan walked in first, heading to the right. Sam followed, pulling her side arm out of its holster. She turned left, carefully checking each room as she went. She went through two bedrooms, a bathroom, and an office. No sign of anyone home. She turned back, checking the living room and kitchen. The house did not appear to have a basement. Rogan met her back in the foyer.

"Anything?" she asked

"Maybe. No sign of life in any of the rooms, and no cars in the garage," said Rogan, "but there is an attic above the garage. Come on."

Sam followed Rogan into the big garage. It was extremely clean and organized. An expensive-looking bicycle hung from hooks on one wall. Another wall was lined with garden and landscaping tools. There was a series of storage cabinets that butted up to a workbench, over which hung a pegboard filled with hooks and hand tools. Rogan pointed towards the ceiling in the far corner of the garage raising a finger to his lips indicating to be quiet.

Unlike Sam's own garage, the ceiling of Dr. Paige's garage had been covered in drywall. It had even been textured and painted a bright white. In the corner, where Rogan pointed, a square had been cut in the ceiling. It was outlined by four thin strips of wood, forming a frame. Dim light filtered down around the edges of the cut in door, which likely led to an attic space above the garage. A long rope hung down from one end of the cutout.

Rogan slowly walked across the garage and put a hand on the rope. Sam followed, keeping her weapon drawn. Sam pointed her pistol up at the cutout attic door and nodded at Rogan. He raised his other hand and counted down using his fingers, one, two, three, pull. Sam jumped back, nearly discharging her weapon, as a ladder came slamming out of the opening above. It made contact with the cement floor, and two rubber-wrapped feet bounced back up a foot before settling down on the garage floor. Sam quickly composed herself, pointing her gun up through the opening. She listened, but no sound came from above.

"Police! Come down now," yelled Sam.

She stared at the hole in the ceiling waiting for someone to emerge. Rogan gripped the ladder and pointed up.

"Watch my back," mouthed Rogan, heading up the steel ladder.

Sam kept aim to the opening. Rogan stopped just short of the top. Slowly, he extended his legs, lifting his eyes above the top of the opening. He turned in all directions. Sam waited, listening hard for any sign of danger.

"Clear," said Rogan, "and weird."

Rogan climbed the rest of the way into the attic. Sam holstered her pistol and followed. The ladder was very sturdy. As she reached the top, Rogan shot his arm down. She took his hand, and he helped pull her the rest of the way up into the attic.

Storage boxes were scattered across the floor of the small attic. Most of the space was too short to stand in. The center was the highest point, where the roof of the garage met at a peak. Sam made her way to the center area, where she could stand to her full height to take in the surroundings. Rogan, with his long legs and torso, had to continue to crouch.

Along the far wall, directly under the peak, a corkboard had been mounted to the wall. In front of the corkboard sat a constructed desk. The top of the desk consisted of a scrap piece of chipboard. The chipboard rested on three five gallon buckets. A fourth bucket was turned upside down next to the desk, presumably as a chair. A halogen lamp hung over the desk, shining a bright cone of light down onto the top of the desk and the surrounding area.

"What do you make of that?" asked Rogan, pointing at the corkboard.

Sam stepped closer to the board. It was large, stretching more than six feet horizontally and four feet vertically. The board's surface was covered with pictures. All of them were of children. Most of the pictures showed smiling children in hospital gowns. Many were lying in bed with IVs in their small arms.

"Strange. Patients of his, maybe?"

"Why would he have pictures of his patients up here? This kind of reminds me of a stalker's nest," said Rogan.

The hidden space did look a lot like the kind of rooms Sam had found in the homes of convicted stalkers and sex offenders.

"Look at the dates on these photos. They range back, what, twenty years?" asked Sam.

Rogan pulled one of the photos off the board. It showed a small brown haired girl waving from a wheelchair. She wore a huge smile, clearly missing a couple of front teeth.

"Cindy, born July 9th, 1984—died, June 23rd, 1992," read Rogan.

Sam knew exactly why those pictures were there. Dr. Paige blamed himself for losing those kids. She looked at all the smiling faces, and she could understand why he cracked. It must be an unbearable burden to have all the skills to save lives, but not the resources. There was nothing to do if the kids didn't get the heart. He felt the transplant program was failing these kids, so he started his own.

Still, Sam wasn't ready to give Rogan the final piece of the puzzle yet. She knew he'd figure it out. She couldn't understand her hesitation, but whenever she thought about telling him about the hearts and the transplanted organs she stopped.

"This guy must have sat up here and stared at these pictures for hours. Look at this spot in front of the bucket. It's stained."

"Blood?" asked Sam.

"No, water stain. I'm guessing tears based on the pattern."

Sam turned from the board and looked at the desk. A leather notebook sat in the middle next to an expensive-looking pen. She picked up the notebook and rummaged through the pages.

"The more I look into this guy, the more I don't understand why he would be killing these girls. And why so brutally? Looking at this board, he was obviously extremely compassionate. What would drive him to kill?"

Sam watched the wheels turn behind Rogan's eyes. She knew he was right on the edge of figuring it out. Maybe his gears were a little rusty after the years of chasing ghosts and goblins. She parted her lips to tell him why, but closed them again looking down into the notebook.

"Listen to this," said Sam. "I lost Chrissy today. She was a fighter. Only six years old. Six years, what is that? I have scrubs older than six years. I am struggling to understand a God that would allow children to die so young. I also wonder how the kids seem so happy and full of life. Is it because they have so little of it?"

"Wow, is that journal full?"

"It's getting there. It seems to be all the same. Dates and names of children that died and then his commentary on what happened and what he would have done differently, or questions about life and God."

Sam closed the notebook and put it back on the table. They would have to get a search warrant to make the notebook useful. She started down the ladder, staring back at Rogan, who was still staring at the smiling faces of the deceased children. *Come on, Rogan*, thought Sam, *put it together. It's right in front of you.*

After making sure they had not disturbed anything in the house, Rogan and Sam drove out of the gated community. Sam nodded at the now-alert security guard as they drove by. They had only made three wrong turns on the way out of the sprawling neighborhood. Sam pulled out into traffic heading towards the Basin. If the good doctor had Darla in his sights, it was likely he would kill her somewhere down there, like the others.

"Well, that was definitely interesting, but we're not any closer to finding him or Darla."

"Can you look up if he has any vehicles registered to him on that fancy thing?" asked Rogan.

"Of course. I can even order up a couple lattes if you want."

"Really?"

"No, you idiot. Hold on."

Sam pulled up the vehicle registration database and input Dr. Paige's information. A moment later, the computer returned one result.

"Looks like he has one car, a late model silver BMW."

"We need to find that car."

"I'll put out an APB."

Sam picked up the radio handset and called into the dispatcher. She requested an All Points Bulletin on Dr. Paige's BMW, asking that if found it be reported directly to her. Riding around with Rogan doing police work felt like riding a bike or putting on a pair of old comfortable jeans. She missed him, his silly banter, his easy going nature, and his green eyes.

Life had not been the same since Rogan ran out of her life. She remembered the day he quit. He came walking in wearing his ridiculous shoes and his old, dirty black trench coat. His eyes were covered up by a pair of aviator sunglasses. His face had a partial beard, and he smelled like booze. Sam sat at her desk watching him. She tried to give him a smile, but he walked past like she was not even there. He went to Captain Cooper's office, marched in and closed the door. A minute later he walked out, walked past her again, and left. He never said a word to her. Never even said goodbye.

Time slipped by as Rogan and Sam took laps around the Basin looking for silver cars. The search seemed futile. The Basin was a big place, with lots of cross streets and alleys. Rogan was not too hopeful about the APB either. The police, especially the patrol cars, had a tendency to avoid the Basin at night. It was an out-of-sight, out-of-mind sort of enforcement. They only went down in the event they were called. Otherwise, the nightlife of the Basin ran under its own set of rules.

Rogan found his mind drifting towards the past. He glanced over at Sam—her ivory skin shimmering under the streetlights, wondering what might have been if he hadn't let it all slip away. They had been great partners, both on the job and off. Then Rogan watched his life fall apart around him. He hadn't allowed himself to think about it, but sitting next to Sam and cruising the streets made him think about all of the things that had happened.

The first one to die was his father, Michael Rogan. Everyone that knew him called him Big Mike. He fit the name. He was just as tall as his son Richard, but with broader shoulders and muscled arms. He taught Richard everything he knew about being a man. Rogan wondered what he would have to say about the last five years. Rogan remembered sitting at The Diner on the morning his dad died. They were eating breakfast, like they had done for years. They were arguing about something, Rogan couldn't even remember what, but he remembered yelling a lot and stomping out of The Diner, leaving his father sitting there. It would be the last time Rogan saw him alive.

That afternoon, Rogan's father was gunned down in the alley behind a drug house. He took six shots from a 9mm pistol to the chest. The police never found the gun or the shooter.

Three weeks later, his mother died. She hadn't been shot, though. In fact, she was the only one of the group that wasn't murdered. She died of a heart attack while writing thank you notes. The Rogans had received hundreds of sympathy letters and a greenhouse full of flowers in response to Big Mike's death. Rogan's mother diligently hand wrote each person a personalized thank you. She had spent days in the study writing the notes. She had even slept in the leather gliding rocker in the room. She had kept the door closed, rarely coming out.

Eventually, Sarah decided enough was enough. She was going to march into that study and drag her mother out. They had barely talked since the funeral. Sarah swung open the door ready to demand that her mother leave the room and the notes and get some sunshine with her kids. Instead, Sarah found her laid over, dead at the desk.

At that point, Rogan and his sister Sarah took a leave of absence. They stayed home for a month in mourning. Sam was great during that time. She stopped by every day to see Rogan and Sarah. She brought them take-out Chinese and rented old Kung-Fu movies.

"Sam."

"Yeah, do you see it?"

"No, I…I know this is way late, but I just wanted to say thanks for being there for me after my parents died. You were great to me and my sister, and I never thanked you for that."

"You didn't need to, Rogan. That's what people that care for each other do. Now, quit digging up old news and help me find the car."

Rogan, nodded, but he couldn't keep his mind in the present. A month after their parents were buried, the Rogan twins, as they were known around the precinct, went back to work.

During their leave, Sam and Rodriguez had been assigned as partners. Captain Cooper gave the twins the option of working together, or they could split Sam and Rodriguez back up and join their old partners. After losing their family, Rogan and Sarah wanted to stick together, so they opted to become partners. For a couple weeks, everything seemed normal. The Rogan twins picked up cases that had hung up while they were gone and solved many of them. Every night Rogan would meet Sam for drinks—and on some nights…dessert.

Rogan started to think that the worst was behind him. Then Rogan and Sarah went down to the Basin to hunt down a serial rapist. They had solid evidence of his guilt and several solid leads on his location. Finally, the last puzzle piece fell into place. One of Detective Rodriguez's snitches saw the suspected rapist holed up in an abandoned factory by the river.

Rogan and Sarah found the factory, and they entered through a side door. It was dark, and the building was huge. They searched slowly through the building until they found the area where the offices would have been. There, in the corner office, they found their rapist, dead. He was laid out on top of an old metal desk with a makeshift knife sticking out of his chest. The body was still slightly warm. Sarah called in the murder, and then they went further into the building to see if they could find out who killed the rapist. They went down a long hallway with many adjoining rooms. Many of the doors were off their hinges, others were missing, and a few were closed. They checked each room as they worked their way down the hallway.

The door at the end of the hall was closed, but light crept out from under the sill. Rogan grabbed the knob and nodded to his sister. She pointed her firearm forward. Rogan pulled open the door and followed Sarah through. The factory floor was well lit from six mobile lighting units. Two long rows of tables ran down the center, and at each table sat a person either stacking money or scooping white powder into bags. Sarah and Rogan had walked right into a drug runners' operation.

Every head in the large rectangular room turned to look at them. Rogan and Sarah stood next to each other, pistols drawn, unsure about what to do next. Rogan pushed Sarah out of the way as a barrage of bullets came slamming past them into the concrete wall behind them. Rogan rolled behind a tall square pillar. Sarah scrambled behind an overturned metal desk. The automatic weapons fire continued, taking chunks of cement out of the pillar and denting the old desk.

Rogan could see that Sarah was completely pinned down. He would be able to make a few moves, but she would not be able to leave her hiding place without drawing fire. Rogan spun to the far side of the pillar, threw out his arm, and took down one of the shooters. As the man fell, Rogan took inventory of their situation.

Six men remained, all with automatic weapons, all closing in on their position. Rogan ducked back behind the pillar as another volley slammed into the pillar. Sarah got off a couple shots and took another one down. Five to go. Priority one had to be to get Sarah to a more defensible position. Rogan rolled out from the pillar again and took out the man furthest to the left. He spun back behind the pillar and nodded to his sister. After three beats, Sarah took off for the set of pillars opposite from Rogan. Rogan spun out and laid down cover fire while she ran.

Sarah made it to the pillar, crouched down, and reloaded. From that point, they took turns firing off rounds at the men, who were now keeping their distance. Rogan managed to clip another man, as did Sarah, leaving only three to go.

The workers had cleared out by now, leaving only Rogan, Sarah, and three drug runners. Rogan spun out to take down another man, but as he did the lights went out. The room plunged into total darkness. The old factory floor had no windows, making the darkness all consuming. Shots came from the men. Rogan could see their muzzle flashes in the darkness, and he returned fire. He had no idea if he had hit or not. He rolled out from the pillar and dove behind the desk. Random shots came his way, and he returned a few randomly placed shots. Rogan ran for the pillar and found Sarah crouching behind the cement.

"Ok?" he asked.

"Fine. What the hell?" replied Sarah.

"No clue. We have to find a way out of here, fast."

Rogan took Sarah's hand. They quickly and quietly ran down the wall of the factory, past the men. Rogan could make out the muzzle flashes as they went by, the men having no idea that their prey had just flanked them. Rogan thought about firing on them, but it would only alert them to their location. Keeping a hand on the wall, they ran looking for a door.

Rogan saw the single muzzle flash too late. It came from up high, from the far end of the factory. Rogan felt Sarah's arm yank down, bringing them both to the floor. He got to his knees, grabbed Sarah around the waist to help her get to her feet, and felt blood. Sarah had been shot. Another muzzle flash from the far end. Rogan flattened to the ground, the bullet smashing into the wall inches above him. Rogan pulled Sarah behind a pillar, took her pistol, spun out and fired both guns towards where he had seen the muzzle flash. He picked his sister up under the arms.

She was still breathing.

Rogan found a door another twenty yards down the wall. He went through with his gun drawn in one hand, Sarah held tightly to his side with the other. He was in a parking lot on the side of the building. Rogan rounded the corner of the building and laid Sarah down on the grass next to the river. Her breathing was shallow. Rogan knew she didn't have much time. Rogan grabbed the phone off of her belt and dialed dispatch.

"This is Rogan. We have an officer down. I repeat officer down. Please hurry."

"Richard..." Her voice was thin.

"Sarah, Sarah, stay with me. Help is on the way."

"Richard...I love you."

"I love you too. Fight, Sarah, help will be here soon. Come on, hang in there."

"Richard...listen to me. I found something. Don't trust kaaaaa...."

"What? Sarah, what?"

It was too late. She was gone. Rogan held her in his arms, rocking her until the ambulance and backup arrived. Two patrolmen had to pry his arms off of her.

Rogan jumped, his body jerking against the seatbelt when Sam's radio went off. He had been lost in his thoughts. His memories were now pouring back to him after all this time. He thought about Sarah's last words. He had never figured out what she was trying to tell him. After his sister died, he shut the world out. He remembered drinking a lot, and recalled flashes of people trying to talk to him, and he remembered telling Sam to go away. Rogan wanted isolation. He wanted to be alone in his sorrow, just him and a bottle of bourbon.

"Stone, here. Go ahead."

"Detective, this is car 698. We swung down through the Basin, responding to a call. We found your car."

"Great! Where is it?"

Rogan scribbled the address down on a piece of napkin. He read the address back to Sam while she typed it into the car's computer. A moment later, a map displayed, showing them how to get to the car. Rogan looked at the map—the area looked very familiar. He stared at the map, concentrating on the blocks and cross streets.

"Amdahl."

"What?"

"He's parked about a block from the Amdahl," said Rogan.

"We better hurry."

Sam turned on the car's lights and sirens. She sped down the streets towards the star placed on the digitized map. The buildings flashed by as she increased her speed. Sam had always been a great driver. When she and Rogan used to be partners, Rogan always had her drive. More than once her fancy maneuvering had saved their skin or allowed them to catch someone trying to outrun them. They had been a great pair, with her at the wheel and him on the trigger.

Rogan wondered if he could even aim a gun anymore. He hadn't handled one since he dropped his on Captain Cooper's desk. The night before, he had polished off a full bottle of finely-aged scotch, then he passed out in the driveway, wearing nothing but a pair of boxers and an old ragged bath robe. The next morning, he woke up to Mac slapping him hard across the face.

"What the hell is wrong with you?" she yelled. "Didn't get shot, so now you're just going to drink yourself dead, is that it?"

He wasn't sure if the swelling in his jaw was from the beating he was taking or the hangover, but Rogan couldn't speak. Mac helped him to his feet, and together they stumbled into the house. She took him to the bathroom and rolled him into the bathtub, bathrobe and all. He was in no condition to protest. She turned the shower on, leaving the water set at ice cold. She saved his life that morning.

After ten agonizing minutes under the stream of cold water, Mac helped him out of the tub. His teeth wouldn't stop chattering, and he shook uncontrollably. She dried him off and threw him into bed, wrapping him in warm blankets that she had put in the dryer while he was taking his freezing shower.

Mac had a great deal of experience in pulling someone out of a good deep drunk thanks to living with her mother. She used her learned skills to snap Rogan out. She told him that enough was enough. He'd beaten himself up long enough. It was time to join the world again. In his selfish spin into the dismal world of depression, he had forgotten that the Rogans had also been McKenzie's family. She had lost family, too. They held each other and cried for several hours. Then they sat and talked all morning about what had happened and about what they would do now.

After the conversation, Rogan got up, threw on some old clothes, and went down to the precinct. That's when he walked into the Captain's office, dropped his gun and badge on the desk and said he was done. It felt odd to once again be chasing down a bad guy, and even odder to be doing it with Sam.

"There's the car," said Sam.

They pulled up alongside the silver BMW. No one was inside. Rogan walked around the vehicle and peered into all the windows. The car was empty. The doors were locked. He considered breaking a window, but he thought better of it. Given the car's location, it was likely that they would find Dr. Paige at the Amdahl Hotel. Sam parked just down the street from the

Amdahl. She clicked a few buttons on the car computer, and a small printer in the bottom of the computer printed out Dr. Paige's driver's license picture.

"Cool," said Rogan.

They walked up to the tall old building. Rogan couldn't believe how much had happened in the last few days. He'd just been looking for ghosts—now he was heading back in looking for a killer. The lobby was busy. Women sat on the various couches and chairs, winking and blowing kisses. Men wandered around the lobby like it was a supermarket and they were looking for a choice ham. Sam walked straight to the front desk. The man sitting behind the bulletproof glass didn't even bother to look over from his crossword puzzle. He just pointed to the tray built into the divider.

"Fifty bucks."

Sam dropped the picture of Dr. Paige into the tray. The man reached over, grabbed the photo. Looked at it, put down his crossword and turned towards the window. Sam slammed her badge against the glass. The man jumped back a foot from the loud bang.

"That man. You see him?"

"Yeah, he comes here all the time."

"Tonight?"

"I think so."

"You think so?"

"It's busy tonight."

"How busy?" asked Sam, playing the game.

"About fifty bucks busy."

Rogan reached into his pocket, pulling out his leather wallet. He leafed a fifty dollar bill out and placed it on the tray. The man grabbed the bill, folded it and placed it in his shirt pocket.

"Well, have you seen him?" asked Rogan.

"Yeah, he rented a room."

"Which one?"

"I think it was the Ben Franklin suite."

"Seriously?"

"Man's got to make a living."

Rogan, sighed and angrily yanked two more fifty dollar bills out of his wallet. The man smiled, grabbed the bills and pulled a key off the wall.

"Have a nice evening," he said.

Sam grabbed the key. The plastic card attached to the key said 519. Sam and Rogan ran out of the lobby and up to the fifth floor. They emerged onto the fifth floor and jogged down to room 519. Rogan took the key from Sam and put it into the door lock. Sam drew her pistol and nodded at Rogan.

He turned the knob and threw the door open. Sam stalked in, covering the room with her gun. Dr. Paige was not there, but the room was not empty. Rogan stepped into the room, and thought he had been transported back a few days. The scene looked exactly like the scene he had discovered in room 416. On the bed, a woman was tied up, her ribs spread out wide. Rogan looked above the bed to read the message.

"To survive, the flock must be thinned of the weak," read Rogan.

"We're too late," said Sam.

"Too late for this girl, yes," said Rogan, "but this isn't Darla."

16.

Karin sat up. She rubbed her head, and her fingers tangled in her hair. Her head was pounding. She prayed for a moment that the frightening events of the previous evening had been some sort of crazy lucid dream. The rope burns on her wrists and ankles confirmed that it had all happened. She was still naked, but the ropes were gone.

She dove under her covers, curled into a ball, and cried. She would go to work, and there she knew she would find a heart on her desk. She worried about Jenny. Her condition was not stable. It would be a poor decision to move her in an ambulance with full medical staff, let alone by a crazy man in Lord knows what. For all she knew Jenny could already be dead—dead like the person whose heart would be waiting on her desk.

Karin got out of bed. Hugging herself around the waist, she walked into the bathroom. The lights worked again. She tried the phone, there was a dial tone. Karin showered, letting the water run down her body while she continued to sob. She felt violated. A man broke into her home, cut her power, and watched her. The man saw her vulnerable, naked, and alone, and he took advantage of the situation. Her wrists and ankles stung under the warm water. She slid down the shower wall to the tile floor, pulling her knees in tight to her face, tears mixing in with the water.

Her head kept pounding, probably from the mix of alcohol and sedatives, but she didn't feel like he had hurt her in any other way. Trembling, she got out of the shower, dressed, and walked around her home checking every lock on the windows and doors. They were all locked. She went room by room searching for some sign that he had been there, but found nothing except a sticker in the corner of her bedroom, where he had sat smoking, staring at her tied to her own bed.

Karin double checked all the locks in the house, and then went to the garage, locking the door between the garage and the entryway for the first time since she had moved in. Before getting into her car, she checked the backseat and the trunk. She waited, tense—at any moment the man could jump out. She got in her car, which started right up. *He thought of every-thing*, she thought as she backed out of the garage. She stared over at the lawn where she remembered being tackled to the ground.

She decided that she needed to meet her neighbors and call to get a security system installed. Her oasis away from it all was no longer a safe haven.

She drove into the city feeling deflated. Usually she took joy in her morning drive, tapping her thumbs on the steering wheel to classic rock, windows open, a smile on her face. This morning she drove in silence with her car doors locked and windows fully up.

Karin parked in her reserved spot and walked into work. This morning she skipped the coffee line. She didn't take the time to look out the windows, and she just barely nodded at the other staff members as she marched down the hall to her office. She paused with her hand on the doorknob, wondering what color the cooler would be today.

She opened the door and sighed in relief when she saw nothing sitting on her desk but her laptop and a couple pens. Karin walked into the room, rounded the desk, and fell into her chair. Gasping, she sat bolt upright, surprised that she had a visitor waiting in her side chair. Detective Rodriguez sat cross-legged in the chair, reading the newspaper. He had placed the chair against the wall behind the door, making it impossible for anyone entering the room to see him.

"Detective!" said Karin. "You scared me! What are you doing here?"

"There was another murder last night, Dr. Gilmore."

"Oh my…" said Karin, trying to sound surprised.

"I'm going to wait here. Hopefully catch the messenger. I hope that's okay?"

"Of course."

"You seemed very relieved when you walked in. Were you expecting something?"

"I…I was just relieved that there wasn't a cooler on my desk like there has been the last few days. I thought maybe it meant that the killings had stopped, that's all."

"I see."

"I'm going to go grab a cup of coffee. Can I get you anything?" asked Karin.

"No, I came equipped," said Detective Rodriguez, holding up a plaid colored thermos.

Karin nodded and walked out of the room, closing the door behind her. The man from last night would think that she called the police. She had to get rid of him somehow. Otherwise the man would kill Jenny. *Maybe he was lying*, she thought. She headed towards Jenny's room. Karin slid open the door to find an empty room. Her heart racing, she closed the door and stopped at the nearby nurses' station. A nurse in bright green scrubs sat at the desk flipping through charts.

"Where's Jenny?"

"Excuse me?" asked the nurse.

"Jenny, room 216, where is she?"

"Dr. Gilmore, she was transferred last night."

"Transferred? What are you talking about?"

"Are you feeling okay? You seem flustered."

"I am flustered. Why would we transfer a high-risk patient?"

"You signed the transfer forms, doctor."

"I did no such thing."

The nurse swiveled in her chair, pulling out a manila file folder from a vertical stack marked To Process. She handed the folder to Karin. Karin opened the folder. It held Jenny's medical record. On top of it was a transfer form. The signing physician on the form was Karin Gilmore. It was her handwriting. She could not remember signing this document.

"Were you here when they picked her up?" asked Karin.

"Yes, I had just started my shift."

"Who picked her up?"

"A couple of paramedics."

"What did they look like?"

"Just a couple older guys, didn't talk much. They just handed me the form, prepped Jenny for transport, and rolled her out," said the nurse, looking puzzled.

"You didn't recognize either of them?"

"No, I didn't."

Karin took the chart with her and walked back to her office. How did this form get signed? She swung open the door. Forgetting that Detective Rodriguez was behind the door, she heard the door clang against the side of his chair.

"Sorry," she said closing the door.

"No problem. I thought you were getting coffee."

"Oh, yeah I didn't make it that far. I have to go over this chart first."

"I see. Here," said Rodriguez, sliding his thermos across the desk. "Try it, it's my own blend."

"Thanks," said Karin, pouring a cup into her mug.

She laid the chart out on the desk, poring over the paperwork, looking for some inconsistency. There weren't any. The paperwork was perfect, as was the coffee. Perhaps the detective had some redeeming qualities after all. Whoever typed up the transfer documents knew what they were doing. She started to wonder if Detective Rodriguez had been right to suspect a member of the medical staff.

The man that broke into her home last night had Jenny. When the heart came, he would find out that the detective had intercepted it, and then Jenny would die. Her only hope would be to catch the courier before he got the heart to her office. Karin excused herself and left the Detective sitting in her office.

The hospital had many entrances. The courier could use any number of them to quickly reach Karin's office. Karin knew that most couriers drove up to the east entrance because the valets would watch their cars for them while they ran in. She decided to wait down the hall from her office in the lounge. She would have a clear view of the east door and her office door. She sat at one of the tables near the entrance of the lounge and pretended to write up notes on Jenny's chart.

Twenty minutes passed. Several couriers had come in, but not one of them carrying anything resembling a cooler. Most carried large envelopes. She decided to go check on the Detective in case she had missed the man's arrival. As she walked towards her office, she didn't even notice the man walking behind her with a small red cooler. Karin opened the door to her office. She could see the Detective's brown leather loafers around the door.

"Karin!" called a nurse in pale yellow.

Karin turned to see a nurse running down the hall towards her. Karin dashed in the direction of the nurse, and they met halfway down the hall from Karin's open office door.

"What is it?"

"Brandon, the kid in 212. His stats are dropping fast, and we can't find Dr. Paige."

"Coding?"

"Not yet, but he needs a doctor very soon."

"Okay, call Dr. Severs from upstairs, get him down here right now to cover. I'll be there in a moment."

Karin turned from the nurse and jogged back towards her office. As she did, she was knocked down by an older man with a gray beard and ball cap pulled down tightly over his face. He was wearing a courier's jacket. Karin scrambled to her feet as Detective Rodriguez charged out of her office holding his jaw.

"Which way?" yelled Rodriguez.

Karin pointed the way the man had gone. Detective Rodriguez took off sprinting, his soles squeaking on the linoleum tiles as he went. Karin ran into her office to see a red cooler sitting on its side on her desk. She grabbed the cooler, unsure of what to do. She should turn it over to the police, but then Jenny would die. Also, the man had already killed whoever this heart belonged to. Not transplanting it would not bring them back, but it might save Jenny. Maybe if the man found out that she did as he asked, even though he was ambushed, he would let Jenny live.

She ran the heart down to the lab, tested it, called the surgeon on call, and proceeded with the transplant.

Karin sat in her office staring out her small slit of a window. She had traded another life. She began to wonder if there was any difference between her and the killer.

Rogan's ears, eyes, and soul hurt after being on the receiving end of another interrogation and disapproving conversation with Coop. Rogan sat with his head in his hands in the interview room with Sam.

"You okay?" she asked.

"No. Another girl died, our suspect is still on the loose. Darla is still out there, maybe dead, maybe not."

"We'll get him, Rogan. One way or another, this guy is going down."

Sam patted Rogan on the shoulder. Rogan felt defeated. He felt like he was missing something. A key piece to the puzzle was eluding him. A piece that he was sure Sam had. For some reason she was not telling him something, something important. Sam's phone began to buzz at her belt.

"Stone," she said. "Woah, slow down, Rod. You're where? Okay, okay…stay with him. On my way."

"What was that?" asked Rogan.

"Rodriguez, he's chasing our suspect. Well, he's chasing someone, anyway."

"Paige?"

"I think so. I'm going to go help. I'll call you when we get him," she said, running out of the room.

Rogan walked out from the interview room and found McKenzie pacing in the same location she had been in when she came to pick him up from his night in jail.

"So is picking you up from the cop shop going to start being a regular thing? If so, I want to talk to someone about getting assigned parking," said McKenzie as she and Rogan exited the building.

"I really hope not. I'm getting tired of being on the receiving end of all the questions. Any news on Darla?"

"Nothing. I called Cinnamon on the way to get you. She hasn't heard anything. It's like she just vanished after leaving the Clinic yesterday. So what now?"

"Well I was explicitly told to stop investigating this and to just go home, so I guess we'll just have to head to the hospital."

McKenzie smirked as she got behind the wheel of her car. "What are we hoping to find there?" she asked.

"Someone that knows where Dr. Jimmy Paige might hide. Rodriguez is chasing him right now by the sounds of it, but that guy couldn't chase down a short bus. He'll lose him. We need to figure out where he might be going."

McKenzie nodded and shot out into traffic as fast as her biofueled beauty could go. Several red lights, honks, and hand gestures later, they parked the blue car in the visitor lot at the hospital. Rogan and McKenzie jogged into the building and headed straight to Dr. Paige's office. The solid oak door was locked. Rogan pounded on the door, just in case the good doctor had decided to come into the office today. The loud pounds echoed off of the floor and brick walls of the hallway. After the second round of futile knocking a woman in a white lab coat appeared from an adjoining hallway. She had light blue eyes with dark auburn hair cut to fall around and cover her ears.

"May I help you?" asked the woman.

"Yes, we need to find Dr. Paige right away. Do you know where he might be?" asked Rogan.

"Well, I'm afraid he is out sick today. Is there something I can help you with? My name is Karin. I coordinate the transplant program, so if you are a family member or a patient, I can try to answer your questions."

"No, we are not family or patients. A friend of ours is missing. We think Dr. Paige might be able to help," said McKenzie.

"Oh I see. I'm not sure how he could know anything about that, but I'm sure he would help if he were available," said Karin, turning to walk away.

"Did you say transplant program?" asked Rogan.

"Yes."

"Dr. Paige, does he work in transplant?"

"He is one of the best transplant surgeons in the country."

Rogan's mind turned over this new piece of information. *Dr. Paige is a surgeon, a transplant surgeon. Is it possible that he was killing these girls to harvest their organs for transplant? Why?*

Because of his shrine…

He had become obsessed. He definitely had access to scalpels, needles, and the Propopental. He admitted to using the services of the Basin. It would not be a stretch to think he would know Dante, who was the perfect fall guy. That book in his office might have been to research how to make the murders look ritualistic. This final puzzle piece removed all doubt from Rogan's mind. Dr. James Paige killed those girls, and he either has, or will, kill Darla as well.

"We need to find him. It is an emergency. Life or death," said Rogan.

"I'm not able to give out his contact information. Hospital policy. If there is nothing else?" said Karin.

"Karin, I don't want to waste any of your time, but I believe Dr. Paige is wrapped up in something very bad. Can we please talk some more, maybe somewhere more private?" asked Rogan.

Karin nodded and led them down the hall to her office. The office was small, but well kept. A small stack of papers sat on the desk next to a laptop computer. One wall of the office had file cabinets running from edge to edge, while the opposite wall had a pair of tall book cases and a slender window overlooking the parking lot. Rogan and McKenzie sat in a pair of guest chairs facing the oak desk, while Karin walked around the desk and settled into a burgundy leather office chair.

"How well do you know Dr. Paige?" asked Rogan.

"I'm sorry, who did you say you are?" asked Karin.

"Oh, I hadn't. I'm sorry, my name is Richard Rogan. This is my assistant, Mac. I'm a P.I. investigating the recent murders down in the Basin."

"Murders in the Basin? You'll have to be more spcoific," said Karin.

"Girls killed at the Amdahl, hearts ripped out of their chests."

"I wouldn't know anything about that," said Karin, shifting uneasily in her oversized chair, the leather subtly creaking.

"I think Dr. Paige does. Did he specialize within transplant?"

"Not officially, but he tends to work with heart patients the most."

"Wow, this is all falling together. Karin, I have reason to believe that Dr. Paige is the one who removed the hearts from those girls. This might sound crazy, but I think he took the organs in some sort of attempt to save his patients," said Rogan.

The needles, the scalpel cuts of the arteries, the demon book, his sudden absence—all signs pointed to Dr. Paige. Rogan was feeling more confident about his idea. Something still felt out of place, though. He turned his thoughts again while he stared at Karin, who was biting the left edge of her lower lip and looking anywhere but at Rogan. Something was wrong, but not with the clues. Something was wrong with this woman. She knew more than she was offering.

"Karin, what aren't you telling us?" asked Rogan.

"Nothing, I, I don't know anything about murders or hearts. Maybe you should go."

"I don't think so. Are you afraid? Did he threaten you, Karin?" asked Rogan.

"I, I can't, please go."

"Listen, Karin, I know you're scared, but a girl is missing. If you know something that would help us find her, you need to tell us. Otherwise that butcher is going to kill another innocent girl."

"You know about Jenny?" said Karin.

"Jenny? She told us her name was Darla. How do you know her?"

"She's a patient, the prettiest little girl, eleven years old. How did you know she was missing? It just happened last night. I've said too much. He is going to kill her if I talk to anyone again."

McKenzie stood up and rounded the desk. She knelt down next to Karin and took her hand. "One of those girls that he killed was my friend. She was going to school to be a lawyer. She wanted to graduate and open a legal aid service down in the Basin, to help people that didn't have enough money to hire a lawyer. She wasn't perfect, she struggled with drug addiction, but she was smart, beautiful, and she would have done a lot of good.

"I know you are scared, Karin, but we need your help. We have two missing girls, your Jenny, and our Darla. Neither of them deserves to be killed or have their hearts ripped out. Whether you want to believe it or not, he isn't just going to hand back Jenny. He'll hurt her just like the others. Your best chance to save them both is sitting in that chair across from you. Please help us, Karin," said McKenzie, tears forming on her flushed cheeks.

Karin slowly nodded. She leaned forward, placing her elbows on the desk and wiping her tears. McKenzie handed her a tissue from a hand carved box that sat on a low cabinet behind the desk. Karin looked with puffy red eyes at Rogan, while McKenzie returned to her chair.

"A few days ago, a heart showed up. There was no paperwork, just a heart in a medical cooler. I should have rejected it, but a girl in the unit took a terrible turn, she had maybe a day left, and miraculously the heart that showed up on my desk was a perfect match, so I looked the other way and had Dr. Paige transplant the heart."

"How did it arrive?" asked Rogan.

"By courier."

"Did you get a look at him, maybe someone that hung around with Dr. Paige?"

"I just saw his back from a distance, older guy, but all our couriers are retired guys who hate being retired."

"Okay, then what happened?"

"The next day, when I arrived at work, another heart was sitting on my desk. Again it was a match to another patient, so again I overlooked it."

"Did it occur to you that these hearts and the Amdahl murders might be related?" asked McKenzie.

"Not at that point. With the hours I work, I don't take much time to watch the news. Later that day though, I overheard a couple of the nurses talking about the murders. One of them said she even cared for a suspect. They talked about their missing hearts, and that is when I started putting it together. I didn't know what to do, though, I mean it might sound selfish, but I could get into some serious trouble for accepting stolen organs. I thought about it all night, and then in the morning, like clockwork, another heart arrived, and I called the cops. I feel so guilty, because maybe if I would have called them earlier lives could have been saved, and now Jenny is missing."

Karin continued telling Rogan and McKenzie about the events that happened since the arrival of the third heart. She told them about talking to a pair of detectives, a woman and man. She described the threat she had received that evening from the killer. She told them how she allowed the fourth heart to be transplanted that morning, even though Detective Rodriguez had been there.

"That must be who he is chasing," said Rogan to McKenzie. "Karin, was he the same man that broke into your house?"

"I don't know."

"The man that broke into your house, did you get a look at him at all?" asked Rogan.

"No, it was so dark, and he cut the power to the house. He stayed in the shadows just out of my vision. All I could see was the smoldering end of his cigarette."

"Did you get any impressions? Height, weight, maybe you recognized the voice?"

"No nothing. He didn't sound like Dr. Paige, but I was pretty scared. Wait though, actually, there was this," said Karin. Karin reached under her desk and began rummaging through her purse. "Here, I found this stuck on the carpet this morning where he had been standing."

Karin handed Rogan a small circular yellow sticker. The sticker had a smiley face smiling back at Rogan.

"We've got to go," said Rogan.

"Why?" asked McKenzie.

"I know who the killer is."

The sun towered above the tall buildings as Rogan and McKenzie raced down to the Basin. The Basin opened for business when the sun went down, so McKenzie had no problem navigating through the narrow, empty streets. McKenzie pulled the car to a halt in front of the Basin free clinic.

"You really think it's that old doctor?" asked McKenzie.

"Yeah I do," replied Rogan.

"But he was so nice."

"The sticker, don't you remember? When we left the clinic he said everyone leaves with a smile and stuck one of those smiley face stickers on our jackets. The sticker is identical to the one Karin found on her carpet."

"Oh my god, you're right."

Rogan jumped out of the car and ran to the door. The lights were out, and the door was locked. A sign hung on the door stating that the clinic was closed for repairs.

"I'm going to run around back and see if the alley door is open or if there are any cars in the lot," said Rogan.

"What should I do?"

"Watch the front," shouted Rogan, running around the corner of the building.

Rogan ran down the side street, dodging a dumpster and leaping over a large rain puddle. His red shoes splashed in the leftover rain from the night before as he rounded the back of the clinic building. Except for loose grocery bags and bits of paper, the back lot of the clinic was empty. Rogan scanned down both alleyways leading to the back of the clinic. He saw nothing in either direction, so he turned and jogged to the back door. The door was locked and made of steel. Rogan pounded violently on the door in frustration. Sighing, he turned away and leaned his back against the door. *What now,* he thought, rubbing his sore hand. Rogan straightened up and turned to walk back down the alley to the front where McKenzie was waiting for him. As he turned the corner, he caught something out of the corner of his eye. A glimmer of light hovered motionless in the shadows.

Rogan turned rapidly to face the light. It looked similar to the apparition he had seen in the Amdahl when all of this started. The spirit had returned. This time it was slightly taller than it was wide, with whispy fibers of light flicking at the shadows of the alley. Rogan felt like the apparition was staring at him, waiting.

He took a step towards the spirit, and it took off down the alley, clinging tightly to the wall where the shadows were thickest. Rogan followed the spirit down the alley, moving further and further from the clinic. Something told Rogan that he needed to follow the misty form, as it easily floated down the alley staying just within view, but no closer.

Rogan felt no fear of the spirit. Instead, he felt comforted by its presence, though he did not know why. The chase continued for another three blocks. The spirit abruptly turned right down a side street. Rogan continued the foot race for another two blocks and then the mist stopped in front of the red door of a small apartment building. Rogan slowed as he reached the steps heading up to the red door. The mist had no eyes, but Rogan felt like it was watching him. He took one more step towards the apparition, and it turned as well as mist could turn and flew through the door.

Rogan slammed open the door and charged into the small lobby. The lobby contained a small set of mailboxes and a singular staircase leading up. Rogan spun around in circles looking for the apparition, but could not locate it. He charged up the stairs scanning each of the three floors as he went up. He reached the top of the building but could not find the misty form. *She had to have led me here for a reason*, thought Rogan, as he descended the stairs.

What significance does this place have? Three days ago she led me to a murder. Today did she bring me to the mur-

derer? Rogan continued to think as he walked out the front door.

He jogged around the building, looking up at the windows high above, scanning for the light. Even in the waning daylight, he could see that only one of the apartments was being lit by interior lights. It was located on the second floor, in the front right corner of the building. Rogan went back inside and took the stairs two at a time up to the second floor. He stood in front of door 2D trying to decide if he should knock or kick in the door. He decided on knocking, in case he was placing too much faith in his foggy spirit. He could hear movement beyond the door, a slow shuffle on the floor. The door creaked open.

"Mr. Rogan!"

"Doc, may I come in?" asked Rogan, trying to hide his shock.

"Of course, of course. What brings you down here? Did you find Dante?"

Rogan stepped across the threshold turning to the side so that his back was away from the old doctor. Rogan had never said anything about going to find Dante. Doc had handed them the belt buckle, but he never insinuated who it belonged to. *Another mistake*, thought Rogan. Just like the needle, and the missed artery, just like the sticker and the clean scalpel cut across Dante's throat.

"Where is she?" asked Rogan.

"Who, young man?"

"Darla. I know you have her."

"Oh heavens, son, I hope there hasn't been some sort of misunderstanding. Darla is here."

"Why is she here? What have you done?"

"I'm just protecting her, son. She isn't hurt or anything like that. I just couldn't stand to see her beat up again, so she has been staying in my spare room for a couple days. She told me about Dante and the beating he gave her, said she sent you on his trail. Did you find him?"

"Yes, he's dead. But you know that."

"Oh! I wouldn't know anything about something like that, but all the same it is not bad news."

"I'd like to see Darla."

"Of course, she's asleep right now in the spare room, but you are welcome to peek in on her."

The apartment had three visible doors. The first was straight across from the entry door. The other two were spaced out to the right. Rogan figured the door that Doc walked towards was a bedroom, then a bathroom, then a second bedroom. The far door would line up with the front right corner of the building, where Rogan had seen a bright interior light shining out through the old window. Faint light crept out from under the sill of the door, and there was an odd blue rug at the entrance to the room.

Rogan turned his attention back to Doc, who walked past a small kitchen and living room laid out to the left of the main door. Doc stopped in front of the far left door and slowly turned the door knob.

"Here we are. Like I said she is asleep, so just peek in, okay?"

Rogan nodded and stepped up next to Doc. Doc opened the door slowly. Rogan leaned into the room. The room had heavy curtains on the window, making the room very dark. A small amount of illumination snuck in through the crack where the two sides of the curtain met. Rogan knew immediately that something was wrong, but it was too late to react. The room was completely empty. No bed, no night stands, no lamps. Just four brick walls and a hardwood floor. Rogan jerked back, but it was too late. He felt something familiar jab into the side of his neck. The soothing warm liquid seeped out under his skin. He fought to keep his eyes open. He blindly swung his arms but slumped backwards onto the floor. Then, once again, everything went black.

17.

"Damn it, Rogan!" yelled McKenzie. "Where the heck are you?"

McKenzie waited by the car like Rogan had asked. She kept her eyes open looking for anyone approaching or leaving the area. She insistently checked her watch waiting for some sign from Rogan. Five minutes passed, then ten. Fifteen was her limit. She ran down the alley. She looked everywhere, tried every door, but there was no sign of Rogan.

She grabbed a chunk of asphalt from the parking lot and lobbed it through the window set into the back door of the clinic. McKenzie reached in, opening the locked door. She stepped into the building. No light came from down the narrow hallway.

"Rogan?" she yelled. McKenzie ran down the hallway, pushing open each door as she went. After checking all the rooms in the back, she ran out into the empty lobby. The building was completely vacant. She sat down in one of the lobby chairs, trying to catch her breath. She needed to find Rogan.

She wondered where he had gone. There was no sign of him anywhere. It was as if he just vanished. She unlocked the front door, walked out of the clinic, and got into her car. She decided to drive around the block to see if he had run off.

McKenzie circled the blocks immediately surrounding the clinic, but she found no sign of Rogan. Her heart beat harder and harder as she looped around the buildings. When Rogan used to be a police officer, she had this same feeling. She worried about him. She wanted to see him come home every day safely.

McKenzie missed Sarah, but even though she and Sarah were best friends, Rogan was the one that was always on McKenzie's mind. She would never admit it to anyone, but she loved Richard Rogan, and not like a brother, even though he was basically her brother. She wondered if that made it weird. She knew he didn't feel the same way. To him, she would always be his kid sister.

Her few friends thought she was crazy to spend so much time with Rogan, but there was nothing McKenzie loved more than spending time with him. She liked going into dark spooky places with him by her side. She liked how he always squeezed her shoulder when she got scared. She liked his eyes. She just wished that he would use those eyes to see that she was a woman now, not some pigtailed little girl that needs protecting all the time.

McKenzie also knew that as much as he denied it, Rogan still had feelings for Sam. She could tell that he regretted how their relationship ended. He basically just walked away, didn't call her, wouldn't even talk to her. During that time, in the weeks leading up to Rogan quitting the police force, McKenzie was the only one he would talk to. She suspected that he only talked to her because she had a key to the house, so he couldn't hide from her.

McKenzie liked Sam—she was a good person. She hoped that if Rogan couldn't be with her, that he would get back together with Sam. They were good for each other. McKenzie made one more lap around looking for Rogan. It was useless; he was gone. She parked by the clinic again, pulled out her phone and dialed Sam's number.

"Stone."

"Sam? Hi this is McKenzie."

"Hey McKenzie, what's up?"

"I can't find Rogan."

"What?"

"We went down to the Clinic, because Rogan thinks the doctor there is the killer, and now I can't find him."

"Damn it, Rogan…Okay, McKenzie. I just got done trying to chase the doctor guy down, but we lost him. I didn't know he was connected with the clinic, though. I'll head that way and start looking. Did you try his phone?"

"It's sitting on my passenger seat."

"Ugh…Rogan," said Sam. "McKenzie, this guy we are looking for is a dangerous guy, maybe you should head home. I'll find Rogan."

"No, he wouldn't stop looking for me. I'll keep driving around looking for him. If I find anything I'll call you."

McKenzie hung up the phone before Sam could protest further. She stared back at the clinic. *Where could he have gone*? she wondered, looking around the grim neighborhood that surrounded the clinic.

Just as she put her car into drive and began to pull away to search for Rogan, she slammed on her brakes, jerking her head back towards the clinic. She could have sworn she saw a light just for a moment through the front window. McKenzie put the car in park, got out and jogged over to the clinic door. She slowly opened the door and walked cautiously back into the clinic.

She could not see any light in the lobby. Heading down the hall, she noticed a sliver of light coming from under the storage room door that Doc had shown them the previous day. She knew that the light had not been on when she was previously in the clinic. Worrying for Rogan and not thinking, she kicked in the door. She had no weapons—only the element of surprise on her side. The door flew open, slamming around its hinges into the wall. McKenzie jumped into the room and struck her best karate pose.

"What the hell are you doing in here?" asked McKenzie.

✳ ✳ ✳

Rogan's wrists hurt, and his ankles, and his head, and most of his body. He felt pins and needles feverishly stabbing his skin up from his feet and down from his hairline. His wrists and ankles hurt in a different way; they felt constricted and raw. He tried to move them, but he felt something tightening against the joints. As the pin pricks prickled up his spine and neck, his vision began to return. He could make out shapes but not features. He felt sure that he was in the empty room in Doc's apartment. He sat facing a brick wall, trying to remember what had happened. He could not focus on any thought for more than a moment before his thoughts wandered off.

His mind was proving unreliable, and he slipped in and out of consciousness. All he knew for sure was that he was in an empty room tied to a chair and that he needed to get out. During his moments of consciousness he could feel light coming from his right, but if he turned to look at the light he became rapidly disoriented and was forced to turn away and close his eyes. He tried to focus on any point in the room, like a small stain on the floor or a particular brick in the wall, it felt like he was zooming in and out on a picture and after seconds nausea would force his eyes closed again.

Rogan found his mind thinking about Mac, hoping that she had not followed him, hoping that she was okay. He did not know what he would do if he lost her, too. She was the last family he had. He struggled to hold her image in his mind. He found it easier to focus on her with his eyes closed than to attempt to focus on anything in the room with his eyes open. He thought about her red hair, layered and choppod to fall sloppily with purpose around her slightly pointy ears. She hated her ears. When they were younger, kids used to call her the red elf, unless Rogan was around. Then they said nothing.

Even as a child Rogan was an imposing figure. His growth spurts hit early and often, so he was always a head taller and much larger than the other children his age. McKenzie's mom had always cut her hair short, because she could do it herself. When McKenzie was old enough to have her own money, she went to the salon to have her hair cut in a way that would hide her elf ears. From then on, no one saw her ears, so no one called her elf, even when Rogan wasn't around. Sometimes though, when she really laughed, one of those uncontrollable deep laughs, she would throw her head back and laugh at the sky. That rare laugh always made Rogan's day, not just because he loved to see her happy, but because when she laughed like that her pointy ears would peek out just for a moment through their red-stranded drapes. Rogan liked her ears—they were one of the many things that made her uniquely McKenzie.

Focusing on Mac, on the small details that defined her, Rogan felt his mind sharpening. He kept focusing on her hair, her ears, the way the edge of her lip curled up whenever she said something sarcastic, which meant that it was curled most of the time. He thought about how her left eye brow would move ever so slightly when she was lying and how she would scratch at her left shoulder whenever she was scared.

After a few more minutes of meditation, Rogan could feel the grog shaking out of his head. He could see, he could think, and he knew he had to act. Lives were at stake, and he was the only one that could help them. He knew Darla was here, and probably the missing girl from the hospital. He also knew that Doc was a murderer. If he didn't hurry, Doc would kill them all.

Rogan pulled as hard as he could against his restraints, but the rope proved too tight. He would not be able to break his bonds with sheer strength. He moved his torso in small circles and heard the chair creak as it supported his shifting weight. *Wood*, he thought. *That is something at least.* Rogan made small movements with his ankles in every direction. The rope burned and tore at his skin, but he continued on until he felt the ropes loosen enough. He pressed his feet into the ground as hard as he could, and the rope dug deeper into his skin as it moved up his shin. After a few more hard presses and movements, Rogan had forced the rope high enough that he could stand at a crouch.

He turned slowly in a circle so that his back was to the brick wall he had been staring at. Rogan took a deep breath and started shuffling backwards as fast as he could, ramming the back legs of the chair into the wall. The legs splintered, allowing Rogan to stand taller. He took several steps away from the wall and took another backwards shuffle run, bashing the chair into the wall with everything he had. The chair broke apart into several pieces. Rogan now sat on the floor amongst the debris.

With a quick tug, Rogan freed his hands and then worked the ropes off of his bloody legs. He stood to his full height, and then stumbled, placing a hand on the wall just in time to keep from falling to the ground. He looked around the room and confirmed that other than him and a shattered chair the room was empty. The only features of the room were a door, a window, and four brick walls. He tugged at his T-shirt, tearing two strips of fabric from the front. He then crouched down and tied the strips around his bleeding shins to slow down the flow of blood.

Rogan lined up with the door, sighed, and took off running towards the door as fast as he could, one step away he leapt off his back leg, throwing his shoulder and entire body weight into the door. He then slid down to the floor, clutching his shoulder. The door did not show the slightest dent or impression that the body slam had caused any weakness. Rogan ran his hand along the grain of the door.

"Solid oak. They don't make them like that anymore," said Rogan to the empty room.

He tried the knob, which was locked. Rogan felt slightly relieved that it was locked—otherwise his shoulder pain would be for nothing. He tried kicking the door knob and around the knob, but the expertly constructed door would not relent.

Giving up on the door, Rogan turned his attention to the window. Save for a shaft of light from the street lamp outside, it was dark. That meant that Rogan had been out for several hours, since the sun had still been up when he got to the apartment. The window had no mechanisms to open it, nor did it slide open. This window was created before fire codes and was just a solid pane of leaded glass seated into the brick. The glass was split into six sections by a decorative matrix of metal.

Rogan walked over to the pile that was formerly a chair and grabbed the largest chunk. Doing his best impression of a baseball pitcher, he hurled the wood at the window. The wood bounced off the glass with no effect. He tried several more times from various distances, but the window held.

Next he returned to the pile and grabbed the longest remnant of a chair leg he could find. Rogan lined up next to the window and swung hard in an arc towards the glass, like a baseball player swinging for the fences. The blunt end of the wood leg made hard contact with the glass and splintered in Rogan's hand. The hard vibrations fired down the chair leg and into Rogan's hands and arms, forcing him to drop the instrument.

Rogan paced around the room in circles trying to figure out how to escape from his cage. If he could get the window open he thought there might be enough rope pieces left that he could fashion a rope long enough to get him most of the way to the ground, or at least low enough that he could make a jump for it and not break his legs.

This will either be the smartest or dumbest thing I've done all day, Rogan thought as he backed away from the window. He bounced up and down like his legs were springs, psyching himself up. He took two long strides towards the window and jumped. His right knee came up to his chest. As he started to descend, Rogan kicked his leg out towards the window with all the force he could muster.

He made solid contact with the old lead pane. For a second he thought it was not going to give, but then he felt his foot burst outwards through the glass, then his calf, his forward momentum stopping with his knee.

Rogan stood on his left foot gripping the window sill with both hands. His right leg was stuck in the glass. His kick had broken just enough glass to get his leg through, but it did not shatter the entire pane. Instead his leg was caught in one of the sections divided out by the thin metal strips that ran through the glass. He tried to pull his leg out, but it would not move.

"Son of a bitch. Now what?"

18.

"Where the heck are you, Rogan?" Sam Stone asked while scanning the streets and alleys in the vicinity of the Basin free clinic. Sam had started looking for Rogan as soon as McKenzie had called her. Sam drove down to the Basin right away in her black, police-issue sedan. Sam tried to talk McKenzie into going home, because the last thing she needed was a frantic girl running around the streets of the Basin with the sun going down. Stubborn as ever, McKenzie declined.

For the last few hours, Sam had been driving up and down the streets around the clinic looking for some trace of Richard Rogan. To make things worse, she had not heard from McKenzie, either. Sam hoped that she hadn't gotten wrapped up in whatever Rogan had gotten himself caught up in.

Sam stopped and asked anyone willing to walk up to her unmarked cruiser if they had seen him. She did not get many takers, and those that did come up were not helpful.

Sam and Rogan used to be a couple, a police power couple. They shared almost two years of red hot romance before the whole thing crumbled. Even though everyone, including Rogan, assured her the sudden end was not her fault, she still blamed herself for the way it happened. Some people still wondered if she and Rogan would get back together, but that ship left port long ago. Sam no longer felt those fiery feelings for Richard, but even after so many years, she still cared deeply for him. She would never tell him she cared, of course, but those deep feelings were why she continued to circle even though she knew that if someone had been missing for as long as Rogan had been missing in the Basin, searching for them usually proved an exercise in futility.

Sam decided to take one final loop. She rounded the corner to extend her hunting zone by one block. She drove past old brick apartment buildings scanning every alley and side street for a sign. She turned the next corner and her jaw dropped as she looked up at a short brick apartment building. She slammed on the brakes and backed up to get a better view of the building. There on the second floor, sticking out of a solid pane window, she saw a red Converse shoe wiggling in the night, spot lighted by the nearby streetlight. There was only one person she knew that wore red Converse shoes.

She remembered the first time she had seen Rogan wearing his now trademark red shoes. Sam and Richard were still in the police academy. The instructor had picked out a young recruit to single out. He made the recruit polish and re-polish his shoes, saying that his police issue black boots were not bright enough. The next day at line up, Richard Rogan stood at attention next to the recruit wearing the red Converse shoes. The instructor walked up to Rogan and looked him in the eyes.

"What's with the shoes, Rogan?"

"Since recruit Mathews' shoes were not bright enough, I decided to find brighter shoes, sir."

Rogan and Mathews were put on cleanup duty in the kitchen for weeks, but the instructor backed off of Mathews. Then, to appease his renegade ways, from that day on, Rogan wore the red shoes every single day and cleaned dirty dinner dishes every single night.

Sam pulled her car up to the curb and ran for the door of the apartment building. She ran up the flight of stairs and stopped in front of door 2D, the corner apartment that would contain the room where Rogan's leg was hanging out the window.

"Police, open up," said Sam, pounding a fist on the door and drawing her side arm. "Final warning. Open this door, now."

Sam listened and heard nothing beyond the door. She checked the knob, but it was locked. She stepped back and kicked at the door, but it would not budge. She put her gun away and pulled out a set of lock picking tools. A moment later she turned the knob, pulled her gun and stepped into the apartment.

The apartment was dark except for a small line of light coming from a door on the far right. Sam ran past the door to the room on the far left, the room with the window that contained Rogan's leg. The door was dead bolted from the outside. Sam turned the bolt, threw open the door, and charged into the room following her gun. The room was empty except for a man standing on the tiptoes of his left foot, clutching the window sill, with his other leg sticking out of the glass window.

"Rogan?"

"Sam! Oh thank you, thank you, thank you."

"What the hell happened to you?" asked Sam.

"No time, get me out of this window."

Sam ran over to the window and broke out the glass surrounding Rogan's leg with the butt of her pistol. He still could not get his leg free. Sam stood behind Rogan and grabbed him around the chest.

"This is probably going to hurt," said Sam.

"I know, but not a lot of options. On three."

Sam nodded, tightened her grip, and placed one of her feet against the wall below the window. Rogan took a deep breath and moved his hands to either side of the window.

"Okay. One... Two... Three!" said Rogan.

Sam pushed off the wall with all her force. She could hear Rogan's jeans tear as they pulled backwards. She fell to the floor, and Rogan's two hundred and forty pounds followed her down. Rogan rolled off of her and jumped to his feet, pulling her up and giving her a huge bear hug. She felt her feet leave the ground as he twirled her around.

"Rogan... Rogan, I can't breathe."

"Oh sorry," said Rogan, letting go of Sam.

"What happened?"

"I'll tell you all about it later, but right now you need to know that the sicko that killed those girls is the doctor from the free clinic. He has Darla and a girl from the hospital. We have to find him and save the girls."

"There was a light coming from one of the other rooms," said Sam.

"After you."

Sam and Rogan ran out into the hallway and down to the door with the light bleeding out from underneath. Rogan went up to the door and stepped onto a blue piece of plastic. He lifted his shoe, which seemed to stick to it momentarily. Rogan looked questioningly at Sam. Sam shrugged and drew her side arm. Rogan turned the knob and threw open the door. Bright light flooded out into the hallway. Sam strode into the room, firearm up. She took aim at a surprised older man wearing a surgical mask, gloves, and gown. In his right hand, he held a scalpel inches above the bare chest of a young blonde woman. Sam recognized her as the sister of the first victim.

"Freeze, police. Hands up, now," yelled Sam.

The man jumped back and threw his hands in the air.

"Put down the scalpel, slowly."

The man complied by placing the scalpel cautiously on a small metal side table as Rogan stepped into the room. Sam scanned the room, keeping her firearm pointed at the man. Darla lay in a hospital bed. She had an IV running into her arm. There was a cooler sitting on a table next to the bed, and a tray with a number of tools.

"Darla, I assume?" asked Sam.

"Yes," said the surgeon.

"Is she dead?"

"No ma'am, not yet."

"What is that supposed to mean?" asked Rogan.

"Well, she would have been dead very soon if you hadn't barged in here, contaminating my surgery suite, I might add. And now Jenny is probably going to die, thanks to you," said the man.

"Jenny?" asked Sam.

"The missing girl from the hospital," said Rogan. "What did you do to her?"

"Me? Nothing. She has a very serious heart defect. Without a new heart my little angel will die in a day, maybe two."

"Your little angel?" asked Sam.

"Yes, she's my granddaughter."

Rogan and Sam shared a look of puzzlement and then both turned back to the man.

"Who are you?" asked Sam.

"People call me Doc, but my name is Dr. Winston Blake, young lady."

"And Doc, what exactly is going on here?" asked Rogan.

"Why a heart transplant, of course. I am going to remove the heart from her and then Dr. Paige there will transplant it into my Jenny."

Sam looked over to where Dr. Blake was pointing. There, lying in the corner of the room on the far side of the bed, a man was tied and gagged. His eyes were closed. He was slumped into the corner.

"Check him," said Sam.

Rogan went over to the man, who Sam recognized as Dr. James Paige from the photo she had printed out of him.

Rogan knelt down and checked his pulse. He shook Dr. Paige, trying to wake him.

"Won't do any good, young man. He is quite sedated."

"But alive?" asked Sam.

Rogan nodded and stood up facing Sam and Dr. Blake.

"You are going to kill Darla," said Rogan.

"Well yes, I suppose that is true, but it's a small price, a small sacrifice really. My Jenny is going to be the President someday. This one here, she'll be lucky to live a couple more years with her lifestyle. Then that perfect heart will be wasted."

"So that is what this has been all about? You have been killing innocent girls to get a heart for your granddaughter?" asked Sam.

"Innocent is a strong word, but no, those other girls were practice."

"Paige wasn't involved? You killed all of them?" asked Rogan.

"Not willingly. I did all of it, he is just here because I know he's the best, and I want the best for my Jenny. It had been a great many years since I cut someone open. I needed a couple trial runs before attempting to harvest the organ from her. See, she's a perfect match for my granddaughter."

"How do you know that?" asked Sam.

"Well, I take their blood all the time at the clinic to check for sexually transmitted diseases. I just started checking for the right bio markers to match Jenny once her condition got worse, and, lo and behold, Darla here is the perfect match. How lucky is that?"

"Luck is not the word I would use. Turn around, hands on your head," said Sam.

Doc turned around and placed his gloved hands on his head. Sam approached Doc, loosening the handcuffs from her belt. She reached up to place the cuff on Doc's wrist. Before she made contact, he whirled around, striking his outstretched elbow into Sam's gun hand. Sam's gun clattered across the floor. Rogan rolled to his right, coming to his feet with the gun trained on Doc, who held Sam by the waist with a scalpel to her throat.

"Now, now son, you put that gun down. Let's not do anything stupid. She'll bleed out before you can squeeze that trigger all the way back."

"There is no way this ends good for you, Doc," said Rogan.

"That's fine. I'm basically dead anyway. Might as well be a bullet."

"What do you mean?"

"Well, young man, I have cancer. Untreatable lymphatic cancer. I'm on borrowed time as it is. All that matters now is Jenny," said Doc, "So you are going to put that down and you and your pretty cop friend here are going to leave. You can come back after the procedure and arrest me or shoot me, I don't rightly care."

"Rogan, you can't let him kill Darla. I trust you. Do it," said Sam.

"Put it down, son. My old hand is getting pretty shaky. We wouldn't want an accident."

Rogan stared at Doc. A man doing horrific things for what he thought was a good reason. His body ravaged by cancer, his granddaughter dying young. He wondered what he would do if the situation were turned. Part of him wanted to drop the gun and let Doc continue on, but he couldn't let Darla die. In this situation, there was no doubt Darla would die, but even without her heart, the granddaughter still had a chance, albeit slim.

"Rogan, do you remember that drug bust down by the tracks."

"Yes, why?"

"I just think it might be applicable to our current situation."

Rogan thought back to that day. He and Sam had found the center of operations for a major drug syndicate. In hindsight they should have called for backup, but being young detectives hungry for the bust, they didn't. Everything went according to plan until a common thug got the drop on them. Rogan stood in a small brick room, about the same size as the room he was currently in. There was a metal desk with a stack of cocaine bricks and banded hundred dollar bills. Rogan stood on one side of the desk, holding a pistol pointed at the man on the other side of the desk, who had Sam around the waist with a jack knife to her throat.

"Good call, Sam. I think there were, what, three in that room?"

"Sounds about right," said Sam.

"Enough! Drop it or I slit her," yelled Doc.

Rogan looked into Sam's blue eyes. He focused all his energy on slowing his breathing and his heartbeat. Rogan shifted his focus to Doc's shoulder, which was just to the right of Sam's ear. It had been years since he shot a handgun. He sincerely hoped it was not unlike riding a bike.

Rogan had fired thousands of rounds through the same model handgun that he now steadied in his palms. He continued to focus on his target, and his training rushed back in. The room began to shrink until all he could see was the wrinkle on the shoulder of Doc's lab coat and Sam's right eye. Sam blinked once. *Squeeze the trigger, don't pull it. Nice smooth motion*, thought Rogan. Sam blinked a second time. *Relax your knees and elbows. Keep your posture.*

Sam blinked a third time.

As her eye lashes crossed, Rogan squeezed the trigger. Time slowed, and the bullet travelled through the air towards its target. At the same time, Sam turned her head and right shoulder towards Doc's scalpel hand, gaining a momentary distance between her throat and the razor-sharp steel. A moment was all she needed. The bullet clipped through her blonde hair, taking a strand with it as it buried itself into the middle of Doc's forehead.

Rogan dropped the gun and dove towards Sam, catching her before she went down with Doc's limp carcass. Rogan and Sam fell into a pile against the wall as the sound of sirens wailed outside.

"You okay?" asked Rogan, turning Sam's chin to inspect her neck. She was bleeding.

"I'm fine, just a nick. Nice shot."

"Thanks, but I missed," said Rogan.

Rogan jumped to his feet and grabbed a wad of gauze off of the side table and held it tightly to Sam's neck.

"You missed?" asked Sam.

"Yeah, I was aiming for his shoulder."

"Oh wow. You need some range time, buddy."

"Is it sick that I missed this?"

"No Rogan, it's not. Like it or not, it's who you are. Thanks for saving my life."

"Anytime, Sam."

Rogan smiled as Sam laid her head on his chest. Rogan cupped his hand around the side of her neck, holding the gauze tightly on the cut, and they waited for the police to arrive. In seconds, pounding feet could be heard on the stairs.

19.

Rogan waved goodbye to Sam as they wheeled her past a set of double swinging doors into the Emergency Room. He still had a problem. Jenny was still missing, and he recently killed the only person that might know where she is. He also needed to let Mac know that he was okay. He felt bad about running off on her. Rogan grabbed at his pookots, realizing that his phone was gone. Either the phone was taken at the apartment, or more likely, it was sitting in the cup holder in Mac's car. Rogan found a payphone in the waiting room. He dialed Mac's number. No answer. He decided to try again in a few minutes.

In the meantime, he had to find a lead for Jenny. He thought of Karin Gilmore. He decided to find her. Maybe she had heard something since they last spoke, or maybe he would get lucky and someone would have found her.

Rogan quickly walked down the halls of the hospital and in-to the transplant wing. He found Karin staring out a window overlooking a pond. She had a coffee cup in one hand and held her waist with the other. She seemed deep in thought.

"Excuse me, Karin?"

"Mr. Rogan! Did you find her?"

"Well we found, Darla, but I am still looking for Jenny. Can we talk, maybe in your office?"

Karin led Rogan to her office, and sat down in her leather chair. Rogan sat across from her in the same chair he had occupied earlier in the day. Karin looked tired, worried. Rogan couldn't blame her. A man threatened to kill her and kidnapped one of her patients.

"Did you catch the man?" asked Karin.

"Yes, we did."

"And was it who you thought, when you ran out of here earlier?"

"Yes, it was. We managed to stop him not a moment too soon. When we ran into the room, he had a scalpel hovering over Darla. He attacked a detective, and I shot him. He's dead. It also turns out I will owe Dr. Paige an apology. He was kidnapped, too."

"Oh my, he is okay?" said Karin, looking worried.

"Yeah, shaken up, but he's doing okay. They are checking him over down at the ER."

"The killer, was he a....doctor?"

"Yes, but he didn't work here. He was the doctor at the free clinic in the Basin."

"Winston?"

"You knew him?"

"Yes, he's the sweetest man. Wow, I just can't imagine him killing anyone."

"Even the best of people snap sometimes. He said he couldn't stand watching his granddaughter die. He decided to take matters into his own hands."

"Yes, he was Jenny's grandfather. You think he was the one at my house? The one watching me?"

"I have to assume yes."

"I am having a hard time grasping all this," said Karin.

Karin stood up and started pacing back and forth behind her desk. Rogan could see tears forming in her amber eyes. Rogan let her make a couple revolutions before continuing the conversations.

"Karin, have you heard any more on Jenny? Maybe some-one heard something?" asked Rogan.

"No, nothing. I found out that I apparently released her. The nurse on duty at the time said two older transporters came in to get her."

"Two men?"

"Yes. Maybe Winston had help."

"You didn't sign those forms?" asked Rogan

"No, well, I mean, yes. It was definitely my signature, but I wouldn't have signed a release form for Jenny. In her state, it is very dangerous to transport her."

It was obvious to Rogan that Doc had to have help. He must have been one of the two men that came in and took

Jenny. It's also likely that he or his accomplice was the courier each time a heart arrived.

That meant that there was still a criminal out there to catch, and more importantly, someone that might know where Jenny is.

"Does Doc have any friends that you know of, people that might help him with this plan?"

"Not that I know of. Winston was one of those guys that kept to himself. Everybody liked him. All I know about him is that he worked very hard at that clinic and didn't get or ask for much in return. I still am struggling to imagine him as a killer."

"Thanks Karin, I'm going to head to the ER and see if Dr. Paige is awake. Maybe he will remember something from when he was kidnapped, some clue that might help us find Jenny."

"I've known Dr. Paige for a lot of years. I'll go with you."

Rogan and Dr. Gilmore walked down the hall towards the ER. Rogan stopped by a pay phone to try McKenizie again, but there was still no answer. He was starting to get worried.

The hospital was busy today. Guests, patients, and medical staff walked or jogged around Rogan and Dr. Gilmore as they strode towards the ER.

"Karin, we went to Dr. Paige's house. He had, I don't know what to call it really, maybe a shrine? It had pictures of children, all of whom had died."

"Dr. Paige is a very passionate, albeit eccentric, man. He's brilliant and yet constantly troubled. He takes every loss of a child personally, like he somehow failed, though there is no way he could have done anything different. Like I said before, his skills are without compare, and the only time someone dies on his watch is if the organ doesn't show up in time. I'm not surprised that he kept a memento of the losses. He always took them so hard."

Rogan nodded as they continued walking. With a hand on the door to the ER, he turned to look outside. A city bus had pulled up to the curb, and a series of passengers boarded. The last one in line seemed to be trying to pull away. Rogan ran out the glass doors leading outside. He could see the girl struggling, and although he was still a distance from the bus, he knew her; it was Darla. She looked over at him and tried to say something, but she was yanked into the bus.

"Wait!" yelled Rogan, running towards the bus. "Stop!"

The bus started rolling forward. Rogan ran with everything he had, but it was too far. The bus was gone. He stopped a block down, catching his breath, and staring at the number etched above the rear window of the bus: G9548.

Rogan jogged back to the hospital, where he met Karin standing outside the front doors.

"Was that…?" asked Karin.

"Yes, Darla, someone has taken her. We need to go talk to Paige now, see if he has any idea where they might be going. I'm going to make a call, though, can you go on ahead and see if he can be woken?"

Karin nodded, and took off through the double doors to the ER. Rogan grabbed a payphone and called Angus.

"Your dime, time to shine," said Angus, picking up the phone.

"Angus, its Rogan."

"Hey bud, what's up?"

"I know you're good with...stuff. One time in a movie I saw a guy track a cab through traffic cameras and GPS. Is that something, a guy of your skills could do?"

"Is this hypothetical?"

"Not really."

"Then let's go with yes."

"Okay, Angus, I need you to tell me where bus G9548 is and where it's going, and I don't have time to answer questions."

"All good, man, I'm on it. Do you happen to still have your earbud?"

Rogan dug around in his jeans pocket. He did still have the small communication device that he used during P.I.T. investigations. "Yeah, I have it."

"Turn it on, shove it in your ear. Save you a lot of quarters."

Rogan hung up the phone and placed the bud in his ear. A moment later he heard Angus.

"Test, test, Ground control to Captain Rogan."

"Angus, I hear you."

"Good, now, I'm going to go out on a limb and say we're chasing the dude that left that body at the Amdahl?"

"Yep."

"Figured, Troll called and told me about your visit. I'm bringing up my...stuff, as you called it. I'll have that bus pinpointed in about five."

"Thanks, Angus," said Rogan, running through the ER doors. He saw Karin talking to a bulky man wearing green scrubs. Rogan ran up to join the conversation.

"You sent him home?"

"Yeah he was fine, and you know how he is, he pretty much does what he wants."

"What's happening?" asked Rogan.

"They discharged Dr. Paige. He's apparently headed home."

"Did he say anything before he left?" asked Rogan.

"Nothing you'd want to hear. Mostly belittled me and the job I did taking care of him. Then he signed his own discharge papers, threw them in my face, and walked out."

"Karin, do you have a car I can borrow?"

McKenzie groaned as she sat up. Her head was pounding. She didn't know where she was or how she got there. All she knew was that her stomach hurt, and she was annoyed. She shook her head back and forth trying to break the cobwebs free. Whatever that freak had given her knocked her out fast and hard. She tried to look around, but she was in pitch darkness. She couldn't see a thing. She felt the cool touch of brick or maybe stone against her back. Her hands were tied behind her back.

Every small movement hurt. She felt like she was on the world's worst cruise ship in the world's worst storm. The ground and the wall behind her felt like it was bobbing up and down, throwing her this way and that. She turned to her side, lurching onto the floor. She tried to remember what had happened. She remembered being at the clinic, and then going into the supply closet. Then everything got real fuzzy.

She tried to stand, but her legs were completely useless. They just crumbled under her weight. McKenzie wondered where Rogan was. Why hadn't he found her? Where had he gone? Maybe he wasn't okay either. *Maybe we should have stuck to hunting ghosts*, she thought as tears began to roll down her face.

Angus told Rogan that the bus's final destination was down in the Basin, but it had several scheduled stops on the way there. Darla and her captor could get off at any point along the route. Rogan drove away from the hospital pulling out into traffic in Karin's car. *Her job must pay well*, he thought as he pushed his foot down on the pedal of the luxury cruiser.

"Okay, now we're getting somewhere," said Angus in Rogan's ear.

"What do you have?"

"I was able to access the security camera on the bus. Lucky for us, they transmit their feed via wireless back to the central bus depot. Piece of cake. I got a view of the whole bus. Who am I looking for?"

Rogan gave Angus a description of Darla and continued to race towards the Basin. He had yet to see the bus.

"Got her. She's drugged up, I think. The cam is black and white, but she's definitely blonde, and she fits your description. She's slumped against another guy."

"What does he look like?"

"Older dude, can't see much of his face, he has a baseball hat on. Blue jacket, wearing gloves. Oh here we go, he just pulled the stop rope. Bus is slowing to the next stop. Corner of 45th and Crenshaw."

Rogan pushed the luxury car harder. He was still six blocks away. He was surprised how well the car cornered as he skidded around the next turn onto 45th street.

"Okay they are getting off through the rear door. He is more or less carrying the girl. Damn, I wish this camera could swivel. I lost them, Rogan. The bus is pulling away. I can't find anything to tap into in that area."

"I'm about there. Call Troll, see if he can get down here. I might need backup."

Rogan squealed to a stop at the bus stop next to 45th and Crenshaw. There was no one in sight. The intersection was right on the odge of the Basin. He could see the bus ahead turning around the next corner. He had not missed them by much. He scanned the area. If they went up or down 45th street he would see them. If they crossed the street, he would see them as well, which meant they had to have gone into one of the buildings on this side of the street. Rogan jogged forward a few paces and saw an alley leading off to his right. Halfway down the alley he saw a door closing.

"Bingo," he said, taking off down the alley.

Without so much as a thought, Rogan slammed through the alleyway door into a dusty old antique store. Broken display cases lay askew at various angles across the floor. A long-forgotten doll head leaned against a post. Bits and pieces of broken furniture and antiques were scattered across the floor.

As he moved into the room, a plume of the heavy dust made it to Rogan's nostrils. He fought as best he could but sneezed loudly. While the dust likely gave him away, it also showed the way. He saw two sets of footprints leading to a stairwell set into the back wall of the old store. One set had confident even strides, while the other dragged and scuffed across the heavy blanket of dust.

Rogan ran up the stairs, taking them two at a time. At the top, he was met with the blunt end of a baseball bat. It slammed into his chest. He exhaled sharply, the wind flying from his lungs. He rolled head over heels backwards down the stairwell, back to the store below.

He rolled onto his back gasping for air. He could hear footsteps descending the stairs as he wheezed. A man stood over him, swinging the bat downward at his face. He managed to get his forearms up in time, deflecting the blow towards the floor. Rogan rolled to his knees and stood. His breath was still labored, but he was mobile.

"You," wheezed Rogan. "I knew it."

"You have been quite the bee in my bonnet, Mr. Rogan," said Dr. Paige, bat raised to his shoulder."

"Where's Darla?"

"Right where she needs to be," said Dr. Paige, swinging at Rogan. Rogan ducked the swing, but Dr. Paige recovered quickly, bringing the bat up and catching Rogan across the shoulder blades. He squatted and rolled forward, trying to put some distance between him and the doctor. Rogan grabbed a piece of a broken tricycle frame as he came to his feet. Paige was on him again, swinging. Rogan blocked the strike, sending Paige whirling with the momentum.

"You're damn fast for an old man," said Rogan.

"An old Marine," said Dr. Paige, swinging at him again.

Rogan deftly dodged the strike, managing to thwack Dr. Paige in the shoulder with the short pipe from the tricycle. Dr. Paige grabbed his shoulder and backed away.

"Why are you doing this?"

"I'm saving lives, you idiot. Not that I expect any of you to understand."

Dr. Paige charged in again, swinging hard at Rogan's head. Rogan could feel the wind flash past his face as he leaned back, knocking the bat to the side with his metal rod. With all his weight moving forward. Rogan grabbed Paige by the wrist, and flipped him through the air. He landed hard atop a glass case, breaking the last of the glass that clung to the lid.

Paige stood up, staring at Rogan. He came in fast. Rogan anticipated the strike but not the direction. Paige indicated that he was going to go for the head, but at the last second he dove downwards, sending the bat right into Rogan's midsection. Rogan tumbled forward to his knees.

He heard a vehicle coming to a stop outside. He looked over—it was Troll's pickup truck. Troll stepped out of the pickup, his monstrous frame easily visible through the dust covered front windows.

"This isn't over, Richie," said Dr. Paige, running out the side door.

Troll came charging in through the front glass. The glass shattered to the floor as he took giant steps into the room. He looked down at Rogan, who pointed towards the side door. Troll took off after Dr. Paige.

Rogan got to his feet, holding his stomach. That last shot had been a doozy. *Dr. Paige must have been a homerun hitter in his younger days as well as a marine,* thought Rogan, stumbling towards the stairs. He made his way to the top and found Darla slumped against a wall in the first room.

"Darla, are you okay?" he asked.

"Mr. Rogan?"

"That man, he tried to hurt me again."

"Again?"

"Yeah, at Doc's apartment, he was there. He stuck a needle in my neck, then he took me from the hospital. I tried to fight, but whatever he put in my neck, I just can't do much of anything."

"It's okay, I got you now."

Rogan helped Darla down the stairs and out into the alley. He saw Troll running back in their direction. Troll came to a stop and picked Darla up. She looked like a child's toy in his massive arms.

"Hi, I'm Darla," she said, rubbing his bald head.

"I'm Troll. Nice to meet you."

"The bad guy?"

"Sorry, Rogan, he outran me, I lost him a few blocks up."

"That's okay, Troll, you probably saved my bacon showing up when you did. I was definitely not winning that fight."

The trio sat on the tailgate of Troll's pickup while Rogan filled in the details of what all had happened. He had a bunch of issues. He didn't know where Paige had gone. He didn't know where Jenny was, and what was even more troublesome was that he couldn't get ahold of McKenzie. He was torn about what to do next. The trail was hot for Paige. He didn't want it to turn cold, but he was really worried that he hadn't heard from McKenzie. He also knew that he had Darla, which meant that Dr. Paige couldn't go through with his plan.

"So what's the plan, boss?" asked Angus in Rogan's ear.

"Angus, I want you to call Rodriguez. Tell him what happened down here, get him looking for Paige. I need to find McKenzie. Troll, can you take Darla home and keep her safe?"

"Nope," said Darla.

"Excuse me?"

"Mr. Rogan, you've saved me twice now. I'm sticking with you. Not because I don't think this big handsome guy couldn't protect me, or anything like that," she said, smiling up at Troll, whose cheeks were turning red, "but I want to help. You said you lost her down here in the Basin. Well this is my place, Mr. Rogan. People will talk to me. They won't talk to you."

She had a point. It was dark, and the Basin would be run by the Basin populace now. It might be useful to have a face that many of the locals would find familiar. Plus, if she was with him, he would know that he had time to find Jenny.

"Fine, we'll all go together," said Rogan.

Rogan locked up Karin's car and hopped in the pickup with Troll and Darla. The old pickup only had a single bench seat, so the three sat tightly packed together as they scanned the streets. Rogan told Troll to head toward the clinic, since that was the last place he saw McKenzie or her car. Rogan stared hard down each alley they passed. He couldn't believe he had been so reckless. McKenzie was missing, possibly hurt or worse, all because he went chasing after a ghost. The ghost did lead him to the killer, though, which was another puzzle he had to solve. Who or what was the spirit, and why did it seem to be helping him?

The pickup pulled up out front of the clinic. Rogan ran up to the front door, which, to his surprise, was unlocked. He ran through the building looking in each room on the way, but he didn't find anyone. He went out the back door, which had recently had the glass broken out of it. There was no sign of McKenzie or her car. Rogan jogged back around the front where she found Darla talking to a woman pushing a grocery cart full of cans. Upon seeing Rogan, the woman turned and took off down a side street.

"Thank you." Darla yelled after the woman.

"Who was that?"

"She stays around here. I see her once in a while when I come down to the clinic. She said she saw McKenzie breaking into the clinic, and then awhile later she saw a man carrying her out and putting her in the back of her car. Then he drove off."

"Did she get a look at the guy?"

"Not a good one. I asked if it was Doc, since she knows him, and she says no, he was too tall and lean."

"Did she see which way they went?"

"Towards the river, she said."

Rogan and Darla loaded back up into the pickup and headed towards the river. They went up and down every street and alley starting from the river's edge and working back towards the clinic. Eventually they got lucky. Sitting between two dumpsters with a large sheet of cardboard covering it was McKenzie's car.

Rogan lept out of the pickup before it had stopped. He tore away the cardboard and stared into the car. No McKenzie, but he didn't see any blood either.

"Is she...?" asked Troll.

"No, she's not here. Check the trunk, though," said Rogan, opening the unlocked door and popping the trunk. Rogan sat in the car, and there in the cupholder sat his phone. He had a bunch of missed calls, most of them from Sam, many more from McKenzie. He pressed her number to call. He hoped more than anything that she would answer and that she'd be okay.

"Mr. Rogan?" said a gruff male voice.

"Who is this?"

"That, Mr. Rogan, is none of your concern."

"What do you want?" asked Rogan.

"Well, as I understand it, you have my heart."

"I'm touched," said Rogan.

"Darla. You have her, I want her."

"That's not going to happen, Jimmy. Nice act back at Doc's apartment by the way."

"Well you just have it all figured, don't you? Doc's idea, he figured if you could find the place maybe the cops would, too. This is all real simple, Mr. Rogan. You have something I want. I have something you want."

"What could you possibly have that would make me want to send a woman to her death?"

"How about a sassy young redhead?"

Rogan felt fire erupt behind his eyes. This old man had just crossed a line. He could threaten him all he wanted, but not her. Not McKenzie. He knew that this was his fault. If he wouldn't have run off, she would still be safe.

"Paige, if you so much as look at her wrong. I will hunt you down and end you just like I did your buddy Winston."

Rogan had hoped that pointing out Winston's fate would throw Dr. Paige off, but if he felt any remorse at the loss of his conspirator, he didn't show it. Dr. Paige didn't miss a beat in the conversation.

"She's pretty, Mr. Rogan. I'm looking at her right now. If you want to look at her again, you'll bring me Darla."

"How do I even know she's alive?" asked Rogan.

"One second."

"Rogan..."

"Mac! Are you okay? I'm so sorry."

"I'm fine. He has me tied up. It reminds me of..."

"That's enough. She's alive, for now. Bring me Darla," said Dr. Paige.

"Where?"

"Where it all began. You'll bring her to the Amdahl. I'll have a key waiting for you at the front desk. One hour, no cops. More than one hour or cops, and I slit this girl open instead."

"Where's Jenny?" asked Rogan.

"She's here, too, waiting for her gift."

"At the hotel?"

"Nice try."

Rogan sat and listened to the dial tone for a few moments. He had put Mac in danger. Why didn't he just stick to hunting ghosts? He'd gotten completely caught up in the case and the way it made him feel. It reminded him of the old days, made him feel whole again. He hadn't even considered that he might be putting Mac in harm's way. He would never forgive himself if anything happened to her.

"What did he say?" asked Troll.

"I bring him Darla or he kills McKenzie."

"What?" asked Darla, eyes wide.

"The man that took you, Dr. Paige. He says if I don't bring you to him at the Amdahl, he is going to kill her. Now don't worry, I'm not going to bring you to him, okay?"

Darla nodded, eyes still the size of saucers.

"When you were with Doc, do you remember him taking you anywhere other than the apartment?" asked Rogan.

"No, just the apartment," said Darla. "Why does he want me?"

"He wants to put your heart into Doc's granddaughter. Apparently you are a match."

"How would he know that?"

"Probably from the blood samples you had to give at the clinic to maintain your pro card."

Darla stared off down the alley. She looked deep in thought. Her brow was furrowed. She started twirling strands of her hair around the fingers of her right hand.

"Darla, I know this is a lot to digest, but I really need your help. Do you remember Doc talking to anyone while you were at the apartment? Maybe you overhead something, anything might help."

Darla shook her head and continued staring.

"Can you tell me what you do remember?"

"I saw you at the clinic, and then I went in to get patched up. Doc said I was real bad and that I shouldn't be out on the streets until I healed up. I told him I could stay at my apartment, but he insisted that I stay in his spare room. He said he would look after me," said Darla.

"So you went to his apartment?" led Rogan.

"Yeah, he had me wait in the clinic, in one of the back rooms. I'm not real sure how long I was in there. I ended up falling asleep. Then we got in his car and drove over to his apartment. He made me supper, and we ate and talked. I thought everything was great. Then, he changed. He said that I needed to get cleaned up. Like I don't know that. Then he grabbed me and pushed me into a room and locked the door. All there was in the room was a mattress, a big bottle of water, and a bucket."

"I'm familiar with that room," said Rogan. "Then what happened?"

"I went through withdrawal. I banged on the walls, I kicked the door. I tried to break the window, but I was trapped. Then another guy came in the room with Doc. I was tired and worn out from trying to escape and fight the drugs. The other guy, he bent down and stabbed a needle into my neck before I could do anything. I tried to fight and get away, but whatever he put in me knocked me out. Then the next thing I remembered was waking up back in the hospital and that same man dragging me onto the bus."

"Are you okay? I mean do you feel okay now?" asked Rogan.

"Yeah, I'm fine, but we need to help her, Mr. Rogan."

"I know we do, but how? I'm not going to hand you over."

"What if we act like we are playing along? I'll distract him, and you two can take him out."

"You'd be putting yourself in a lot of danger, Darla."

"It's okay. You saved my life. I owe you one. Plus, we have Troll on our team."

"I can't let you do that."

Darla smiled at Rogan with her lightly stained teeth. Rogan imagined what she might have been like if she hadn't fallen in with the Basin crowd. He could see strength in her, and beauty. She turned and started walking down the alley.

"Where are you going?" asked Rogan.

"I'm on my way to the Amdahl. I know you don't want anything to happen to me, so you might want to tag along."

20.

Troll parked a block away from the Amdahl. They walked together into the lobby and approached the front desk. A different man was manning the helm today. This one was reading a book instead of paying attention.

"Fifty bucks."

"I have a reservation, under Rogan."

The man sat his book down, using a gum wrapper as a bookmark. He picked up a key on the back desk and slid it through the portal to Rogan. The key read 616. The room Rogan and McKenzie had investigated just days ago.

Rogan, Darla and Troll walked up the six flights to the sixth floor. The floor seemed different tonight. There were no cameras and detectors placed out in the halls, no cables running along the floors. The noise of people taking care of their personal business resonated along the hallway. The three came to a stop in front of 616. Troll nodded at Rogan and took up a position next to the door.

"Thanks for doing this, Darla."

"No problem. I know what she means to you. If I had a boy-friend I'm sure I'd do about anything to save him."

"Oh, Mac isn't my girlfriend."

"Really? Wow, could have fooled me."

Rogan stared at Darla for a moment and then unlocked the door to 616 and stepped inside. The room was dark and emp-ty. He turned on the light. The painting over the bed still hung askew.

"No one's here," said Darla.

"Yeah, I noticed."

Rogan walked around the room. He checked the bathroom. He and Darla were definitely the only people in the room. Rogan was about to leave when he heard the theme to _Ghost-busters_ coming from his pocket. He pulled out his phone, the screen indicating that the incoming call was coming from Mac.

"Hello."

"I'm impressed," said Dr. Paige.

"Where are you?"

"No concern of yours."

"How do you know I'm at the hotel?"

"Smile towards the door."

Rogan looked over and saw a small camera sitting on the door ledge. It looked to be wireless—able to transmit data across the internet, meaning that Dr. Paige could literally be anywhere.

"Curiosity, how did you get her there?"

"Given her career, I told her she owed me one for saving her life."

"Good thinking, young man. In the drawer by the bed, you'll find a syringe. Have Darla lie on the bed, put that in her neck and squeeze. Then you leave."

"Where's Mac?"

"She's here. Give Darla the sedative, leave the hotel, and go home. Once I pick up Darla, I will call you and tell you where to find your pretty friend. If I do not get to safely pick up Darla, your friend will die, slowly, from dehydration and hunger."

"I need to know she's still alive before I do this."

"Fine."

"Rogan, in case I die, my account number is 122915," said McKenzie.

"Enough! Do it, or I kill her," said Dr. Paige.

Rogan hung up the call, smiled, and turned to Darla. McKenzie had just given him a clue. He couldn't tell if the camera had speakers. He sat on the edge of the bed near the open drawer with the syringe. He would need to make this look good. He had to buy some time.

"Darla, come over here."

Darla walked over and stood in front of Rogan, looking at him with confusion in her eyes. She was rubbing her elbows just like when he had first seen her. She was wearing the same thin white shirt, too. She blew wispy strands of hair out of her mouth. Her eyes darted back and forth around the room.

"Straddle me."

"What?"

"Just do it."

Darla put one slender leg along each side of his waist, kneeling on his lap. Rogan pulled her in close, putting his mouth next to her ear away from the camera. She felt fragile in his arms. Her thin legs squeezed against his thighs. Her flat chest pressed against him as he tightly wrapped his arms around her boney back.

"He wants me to stick you with that needle in the drawer. I'm not going to do that, but we need to make it look like I did. Once I pull that needle out, I'm going to need you to fight me a little bit. Then I'm going to pretend to inject you, okay?" whispered Rogan.

"Got it. Roll me on my back—that will be more believable," whispered Darla.

Rogan rolled, putting Darla on her back. She wrapped her legs around his back, holding him tightly against her. Rogan took his right hand and reached into the drawer, withdrawing the syringe. He held it up high, making sure that it would be visible in the camera.

Once she saw the syringe, Darla punched at Rogan's chest, rolled, and tried to crawl away. Rogan grabbed her and pulled her back under him. He straddled her waist. She screamed out as he pressed her to the mattress. She wiggled and squirmed under his weight, throwing her head back and forth. He moved up her body, pinning her arms down. He took his left hand and held her head still. With his right, he punched the syringe into the mattress millimeters from her neck. She continued to fight, then slowed, then lay completely still.

Rogan was impressed with her act. He just hoped that Dr. Paige had bought it.

"Okay, now lie real still for ten minutes, and then get the hell out of here. Troll will take care of you. Thank you, Darla," Rogan whispered into Darla's ear.

Rogan walked over and held the syringe up to the camera, showing that it was empty. Then Rogan walked out of the room and slammed the door as hard as he could. He listened and heard the camera ping off of the floor.

Troll looked at him, puzzled.

"Everything okay?" he asked.

"Yeah, Darla is pretending to be sedated. She is going to wait ten minutes and then come out. You watch after her, okay?"

"Will do."

"Angus, did you pick up on McKenzie's clue?"

"Yep, sure did. Smart girl that one."

McKenzie was indeed a smart girl. She had given them a hint, a coded hint that would sound like nothing to anyone else, but he knew exactly what she meant. The number she rattled off sounded like a P.I.T case number.

"Got it pulled up. Oh yeah, you don't remember this joint? Old nut house down in the Basin? There was hella activity up in there."

"The Porter House?"

"Yeah, down by the river."

"Thanks, Angus," said Rogan, charging down the stairs.

The Porter House had been a psychiatric care facility. It had been shut down over fifty years ago because of questionable practices by the doctors in residence there. The reports stated that the doctors in the hospital, especially its namesake, Dr. Porter, used any number of gruesome torture techniques to rid patients of their mental ailments. The experiences P.I.T. had at the facility were shocking. They saw various shadowy figures, heard screams. They even witnessed a desk moving across the floor. The place was without a doubt one of the most haunted places Rogan had encountered. Could Dr. Paige have taken Mac there? She had spent a lot of time in the building with Rogan, scouting the location before they did the investigation. A couple flights from the bottom, Rogan flipped his phone open again and dialed the hospital. He asked for Karin Gilmore.

"Dr. Gilmore."

"Hi, Dr. Gilmore, this is Richard Rogan."

"Oh! Do you have news?"

"Yes, I know where Jenny is. I need you to send an ambulance to the Porter House down by the river in the Basin."

"The Porter House? Oh my...I will send them down right away."

Rogan closed the phone, jogged through the lobby, and out into the night air of the Basin.

"Time to end this," said Rogan.

"Damn. My camera fell," said Dr. Paige.

"Oh, no more peepy show for grandpa?" mocked McKenzie.

Dr. Paige shot McKenzie a look and then walked over to the far table in the small brick room. The room was in the basement. It was cold and completely lacking in modern lighting. Dr. Paige had to carry in halogen lights to light the dreary room. The walls had been painted a dull brown. The floor was poured cement, and there was a grate in the middle of the floor. McKenzie knew from her research that the grate in the floor had been used to drain blood.

There were two metal tables in the room with a large machine secured to the floor in between them. It had taken McKenzie a lot of time searching through dusty records to find out what the machine had been used for. In essence, it was one of the first blood transfusion machines. The idea had been that deep psychosis was in the blood. If the blood could be cleansed, then the patient would recover. The machine would be hooked up to the patient, and their blood would be drained through the machine through a special filter designed by Dr. Porter himself, and then returned back to the patient.

The room had also been used to perform simulated drowning, bloodletting, and extended periods of hanging upside down. It was Dr. Porter's belief that mental illness had a biological basis and could be solved by manipulating the body.

One of the tables was empty. The other had a thin pad and a young girl.

"So what's the end game here, Paige? You're just going to go get Darla, bring her back here, and put her heart in that girl? Then what?"

"Then Jenny lives."

"Why do you care?" asked McKenzie.

"I made a promise to help her. You know the doctor at that crappy clinic where you found me?"

"Yeah?"

"Jenny is his granddaughter."

So Rogan was right after all, thought McKenzie. He just hadn't considered that the psycho killer fest might have been a team effort. She had been glad to hear his voice. She'd thought maybe Doc had gotten the drop on him. She didn't know what she'd do if she lost Rogan.

"Doc was involved?"

"Oh, yes. His name is actually Winston. I think it's ridiculous that he makes everyone call him Doc. Without him, though, none of this would have been possible, which is why I owe it to him to finish the job."

"What do you mean?"

"We were drinking together one night. See, I've known Winston a long time, so we went out for beers once in a while. He told me about his cancer and how he wished there was something he could do for his granddaughter before he died. We left it at that, but the next time we went out I made him a deal. I said, 'Winston, if you supply me with the names of working girls that match these biomarkers, I will get your granddaughter a heart.'"

"So he decided who you should kill?"

"Who to harvest from, you mean. Well, we decided by their blood. Winston gave all of them blood tests, you see, so they can keep doing their work. I supplied the high risk patient list to Winston, and he compared it to the hookers that frequent the clinic. Now that he's dead, I have to take things into my own hands. I have to finish our work."

"If you were working with Winston, why did you help us when we came to see you at the hospital? That report led us straight to him."

"That was part of our contingency plan. If someone came snooping around the hospital, I would send them to him, and he would in turn send them to Dante, whose record and way of life should speak for itself. We figured the pimp would keep the cops busy for a while."

"So why kill him?"

"Dante? That one was Winston. I just wish he would have waited a little longer. The plan was for the cops to waste time questioning him, but it seems they found him dead when they got there. Winston said he left a suicide note, but that was sloppy, in my opinion. He was just so worked up that Dante beat on Darla. He snapped and went over there."

"So he killed Dante, and you killed all those girls?"

"Yes. It was a lot easier than I thought. Once I got that first one done, it actually kind of turned out to be fun. Darla is supposed to be the last one. I was going to kill her too, but Winston insisted on harvesting the organ for his granddaughter."

McKenzie wondered what happened with Doc. Rogan, as a general rule, didn't kill people without a really good reason. She had to keep Dr. Paige talking, keep him distracted. She knew that Rogan would pick up on her hint. She knew that he would come for her, and she wanted to make sure that Dr. Paige was here to get caught as well.

"But you're going to kill Darla. No matter what you want to call it, you and Doc killed those other girls too. They didn't deserve that."

"Do you know how sickening it is to patch up those whores just so they can go out and get beat on again? Or to see a girl with a perfectly good heart stuff her veins with drugs while your patients fight for their lives? What they don't deserve, young lady, is their lives."

"You're a doctor though; didn't you take an oath or something to do no harm?"

"I've been a doctor longer than you've been alive. I discovered years ago that doing no harm didn't always work. For years I've watched children, woman, daughters, sons, fathers, and mothers die because they needed a heart transplant. I had to just sit there and watch them die; there was nothing I could do about it. Not a damn thing. It's not fair, those people, especially the kids. They have so much life ahead. How could I not do something? It took me a long time to come to the realization of what I had to do. I needed to save them. I had to, no matter the cost. That's when I came up with this idea, and then Winston came along, and it all fell into place. We could have saved a lot more lives too if you and that Rogan wouldn't have come sniffing around. I had the cops off on tangents, but you two..."

McKenzie heard a creaking door down the hallway. She wondered if Rogan had arrived. She knew he would get there as quickly as he could, but it was too soon for him to have covered the distance. More likely the former residents of the Porter House were waking.

"What was that? Did you hear that?" asked Dr. Paige.

"I told you, this place is haunted."

McKenzie remembered hearing a lot worse than a creaking door when they were here last. She wondered when the real noises would begin. Dr. Paige ran his hands through Jenny's hair. She was unconscious. He looked around the room pensively. The sound of a glass bottle shattering on the floor echoed down the hall.

"What about Karin Gilmore?" asked McKenzie.

"What about her?"

"We talked to her. She said someone broke into her house and threatened her. Was that Doc, I mean, Winston?"

"No, no, that was me. Winston's far too old to pull that off."

"But Karin found a sticker on the floor in the bedroom. A yellow smiley face sticker. We got the same sticker when we went to talk to Doc at the Clinic."

"Oh yes, him and those damn stickers. He stuck one on my coat before I went over there. Must have fallen off. Is that what led you to him?"

"Yes. Before that, we thought it was you, to be honest."

"Really? I thought I covered my tracks pretty well."

"No, you really didn't."

"Wow, what was that?" asked Dr. Paige, jerking his head towards the door. "Okay young lady, you've kept me talking long enough. I have to go get Darla's heart."

Dr. Paige zipped up a leather bag and grabbed a blue cooler. He put on a brimmed hat and leather gloves. He grabbed the door handle and swung it open. He grasped the front of his hat with his thumb and forefinger, nodding towards McKenzie.

"If she's not there, I'm afraid I'll be back to kill you. You will want to hope there is a smile on my face when I come back through that door," said Dr. Paige, walking out of the room and closing the door behind him.

McKenzie smiled and worked the scalpel out of her sleeve that she had lifted off of Dr. Paige earlier. Her pickpocketing days may have been a bad time in her life, but the skills she learned continued to come in handy. She began to work at the ropes with the sharp edge. She had to get free and call for help.

Rogan sprinted away from the Amdahl towards the river. The Porter House was only about three blocks from the old hotel. Rogan knew the place well. The building was large, with many windows but only one door. Rogan knew where Paige would be, though. There was only one place that could possibly be set up to transplant a heart. The sign on the door said Advanced Treatment Techniques, though based on the reports and research documents Rogan read, it should have been marked as the torture room. Rogan continued to run, his legs throwing long shadows under the street lights. Each pounding stride sent pain firing up Rogan's injured legs.

Out of breath, he ran up to the gate of the Porter House. The building was completely dark. Rogan knew that the torture room was in the basement. He wondered if Dr. Paige had started to hear the voices and cries yet.

Rogan ran up to the building and crawled through a broken window on the ground floor. It was the same window P.I.T had used to gain entrance to the facility after being denied access by the current property owner. He ran downstairs and ducked into one of the side rooms as he saw Dr. Paige exit the torture room at the end of the hall. Dr. Paige was carrying a cooler and looked flustered. Apparently the Porter House guests had begun to welcome him. Rogan hid in the corner, ready to take out Dr. Paige as he went by. Through the small gaps in the old wall, Rogan could see Dr. Paige coming. He picked up a piece of busted wood and waited. One door down from Rogan, Dr. Paige abruptly stopped.

"Damn," said Dr. Paige.

Dr. Paige turned and sprinted back to the torture room. Rogan couldn't figure out why. Then he listened and heard the sirens outside. It sounded like several vehicles. Rogan could pick out one ambulance for sure and three police vehicles. If they stormed this place it would be likely that Dr. Paige would use McKenzie as leverage, possibly even kill her.

Rogan snuck back out of the building and ran down the driveway. There he found Karin Gilmore with two paramedics and Detective Rodriguez with three squad cars.

"Rogan! What are you doing?" asked Rodriguez.

"Trying to save Mac. I was just about to take the guy out when you guys came blaring up here. Now he has himself locked in a room with one entrance and two hostages."

"Okay, thanks for the intel; we'll head in, flush him out."

"If you go charging in there, Rod, you know there is a good chance he kills those hostages," said Rogan.

"You have a better idea?"

"Yeah, let me go back in. I'll have him running out. Give me ten minutes, that's all I'm asking."

"Men, let's get this place surrounded. I want eyes on all exits. Fine. Rogan, you have ten minutes. Take that long for the hostage negotiator to get here anyway. How do you know you can get him out of there?"

"Because he's in my world now," said Rogan, walking back to the broken window.

Dr. Paige paced back and forth across the small room. He looked down at Jenny. They were so close to having this finished. She would have a new heart, and he could head off. Before the cop cars pulled up he had assumed that only this cute redhead and Richard Rogan knew he was involved. He figured he could do the transplant, kill McKenzie, and then just wait for Richard Rogan to show up and kill him too. Now there were cops outside, cutting him off from the heart. It would have been so easy! He had even figured out how to get the old bypass machine working, and he had spent hours sterilizing it and the room. Everything was perfect. Now he had to deal with cops. He heard a clanging from down the hall.

"The longer we're here, the worse it's going to get," said McKenzie.

"I think I'll take ghosts over cops. Ghosts can't hurt me."

"I wouldn't be so sure of that. When we were here last time, Travis, a guy on our team, was in this room. He sat on the empty table there, and something grabbed him. He had a bruise around his wrist when he came out."

"Really?"

"Yeah, this place is no joke, Doc."

"Mooooaaannn…" A voice echoed down the hall.

Dr. Paige didn't believe in ghosts. He was a man of science. He knew that there was no plausible way ghosts could exist, and he certainly knew that they couldn't hurt him.

Dr. Paige went over to the door, opening it a crack. He peered down the hallway, looking for the source of the commotion. He watched a small wheel, likely from an old hospital bed, roll towards him, stopping when it hit his foot. Dr. Paige could feel his heart rate rising. What was going on? He had to get out of here, but what about Jenny? He couldn't take her with him—she was far too unstable to move quickly. She would be brought back to the hospital. If he got the heart, maybe he could convince Karin to put it in. He had scared her enough to make her transplant the fourth heart. Maybe with a little push she could be persuaded to do it just one more time.

"Doooooctooooor…"

Dr. Paige slammed the door, putting his back against the wood. His chest rose and dropped rapidly as he looked over at McKenzie.

"You know, these people were tortured by doctors. Many were killed in extreme experiments," said McKenzie.

"I've got to get out of here. There has to be another way out."

"Front door is the only way I know. It was a controlled facility, and fire codes weren't an issue back then," said McKenzie.

"Has to be another way," said Dr. Paige.

Dr. Paige opened the door again and walked into the hall. He would not let some voices and a little banging around scare him. He would find another way out, a window or something. Some way out where he could get away and then get to the Amdahl before Darla woke up. Dr. Paige slowly walked down the hallway, clutching the cooler to his chest. From his left, he heard metal clanging. He focused on his breathing and walked forward.

"You're going to die, dooooctoooorrrr…" said a gravelly voice from behind him.

Dr. Paige spun around, but there was nothing there. He could see the stairway just another twenty yards away. He took a few more steps and felt someone grab his shoulder. He spun again, but no one was there. He grabbed his shoulder. It hurt. Whatever grabbed him had a vice-like grip.

"I don't want any trouble. I just want to get out of here," said Dr. Paige.

Dr. Paige could hear giggling coming from all around him. He wiped sweat from his brow and began to run towards the stairs. He felt several small projectiles smack against his back as he made the first stair. Dr. Paige ran up the stairs, ending up in the lobby. He could see the flashing lights through the lead glass windows of the front door. He turned away from the door and headed towards the back of the building. He ran down a long hallway with rooms on either side.

Off to his left he could hear something scraping against the floor. The hallway ended in a T. As he approached the end, a rusty wheelchair rolled by. Then he felt a tap on his left shoulder. He turned, but again no one was there. He stood at the end of the hall with his back against the wall, scanning back and forth down the three hallways. Out of the corner of his eye he saw a shadow moving down the hallway to the left. He could hear chains rattling to his right. His heart raced faster.

"Doooooctooorrr...play with us. ...dooooctooooorrrr," said small female voices.

"Shut up, leave me alone. Leave me alone. Please just stop," said Dr. Paige.

Dr. Paige dropped the cooler. It bounced off the floor, and the noise echoed down the hall. He could hear the laughing again all around him. He saw the shadows move. He heard scraping on the floor. It sounded like it was growing louder, getting closer. He looked down at his hands, they were trembling. He had never been so scared in all his life. He could see no windows, no doors on the backside of the building. He felt hopeless.

Several items clanged off the wall next to him, just a few feet away. He looked down to see three rusty scalpels lying on the ground. He screamed and ran back down the hallway. Dr. Paige ran back into the lobby and burst out through the front door. He stumbled down the stairs and rolled onto the gravel driveway. Within seconds, two police officers were on him, putting his hands behind his back. They dragged him to a car and shoved him into the backseat. He couldn't stop shaking.

Dr. Paige looked out the window back at the frightening old building. He saw a ghost standing in the second floor window waving to him. He looked again, concentrating on the form behind the tall, leaded glass window. It was not a ghost—it was Richard Rogan. He jerked his head down a floor and one window over as a shadow passed by. The shadow stopped and stared at him with crossed arms. *The girl! How did she get loose?*

✳ ✳ ✳

Rogan laughed as he waved at Dr. Paige in the backseat of the cruiser. That had been easier than he had expected it to be. He sprinted down the stairs to the basement. To his left he thought he saw a shadow. The shadow stopped in the window. It was female shaped. No, it was McKenzie shaped.

"Mac!"

The two ran towards each other. Rogan grabbed McKenzie and held her tight. Rogan loosened his grip and took a step back, leaving his hands on McKenzie's shoulders. He looked her over—she seemed unharmed except for some rope burns on her wrists.

"You okay, Mac?"

"Yeah I'm fine. Paige looked freaked when he ran out of here."

"Yeah, I'm guessing you had something to do with that?"

"Maybe a few subtle hints to get the ball rolling. Then I saw what you were doing, and I couldn't let you have all the fun," said McKenzie, smiling.

"Nice work on the kid's voices by the way. I almost ran out myself—way creepy."

"Thanks. We should go check on Jenny, make sure she's okay."

Rogan nodded. Together they ran down to the torture room. As Rogan gripped the door handle, the hairs on the back of his neck stood on edge. They were not alone. He turned slowly, but he did not see anything. There was a soft moan in the distance. Rogan shook his head, getting his focus back. He pulled open the door.

"Man, I hate this place," said McKenzie.

"Tell me about it. I feel like we only did about a third of the scaring out there."

Rogan and McKenzie walked across the cement room to the table with the small girl. She looked peaceful, with an IV in her arm and an oxygen mask over her small face. McKenzie reached down and checked her pulse.

"She's okay. Breathing and beating," said McKenzie.

Rogan put his arm around Mac's shoulders, and they walked out of the room as the paramedics ran in. Rogan and Mac walked up the stairs and out through the lobby door. Rodriguez met them in the driveway.

"Spill it, Rogan. How did you do that? That guy is scared out of his mind."

"You should come on a hunt with us sometime, Rod. It's absolutely amazing what the mind can come up with with just a little persuasion."

"Rod, you're going to need this, too," said McKenzie, pulling out a digital recorder from her jacket pocket.

"What's this?" asked Detective Rodriguez.

"His confession. I turned on the recorder when he nabbed me. It's all on there. I kept him talking, and he spilled everything."

"Nicely done, Red."

"That's my partner," said Rogan, throwing his arm once more around McKenzie. Together they walked down the gravel driveway of the Porter House, past the flashing lights and away from the haunted asylum. Rogan felt exhausted, but elated. The case was solved and, more importantly, McKenzie was safe.

21.

The next morning, just like most mornings, Richard Rogan sat at his Diner eating the same exact breakfast he had eaten every day since his father had been killed. He stared at the impression in the seat wondering where to go from here. Mac walked in as Rogan contemplated.

"Scoot," said Mac, sliding in next to Rogan.

"You okay?" asked Rogan.

"Peachy. Everyone else okay?"

"Yeah, Sam's fine. She lost quite a bit of blood, but they got her all patched up. Darla called this morning. She packed up her stuff and has moved out of the Basin. She's headed east to stay with some relatives while she tries to find safer work."

"So it all worked out."

Rogan nodded, twirling the big gold ring on his finger. It did all work out. The bad guys were dead or in jail, and the good guys were alive, except for the girls the two psycho docs killed. Rogan wished he could have solved the puzzle faster; maybe he could have saved a couple of them from dying like that.

"It's kind of a heartbreaker when you think about it," said McKenzie.

"Pun intended?"

"Perhaps, but it is. I mean there's Doc, who just wanted to save his granddaughter before he died. Killing people was probably not the best way to go about doing that, but he just wanted to save her. Then at the end it was all for nothing. He's dead, and his granddaughter still needs a heart."

"Well maybe old gramps had some influence from beyond the grave. I called Karin earlier to see how Jenny was doing, and she told me that it was an exciting day. A heart had shown up, with proper paperwork this time. Apparently, there was a major traffic accident a town over, and amazingly one of the organ donors is a match for Jenny."

"Really? She's going to make it?"

"Sounds that way."

"Wow, that's amazing. Goes to show you sometimes life has a funny way of working out. Maybe Doc was right; maybe she is our future president."

"Well hopefully she won't grow up like her grandfather."

"Oh come on, Rogan. Have a heart."

"Really, you're going there?"

"You know I had to."

They sat in silence for several minutes. Edna delivered a cup of hot water and a packet of earl grey tea for McKenzie.

He could hear Delores humming in the kitchen. Rogan looked around the Diner. They were the only patrons, which should have concerned Rogan, since he owned the place.

He'd purchased The Diner with some of the life insurance money he received after the deaths of his family members. He could not bear the thought of it ever closing down. He and his father had eaten breakfast in The Diner every day for as long back as Rogan could remember. His dad, in his camel-colored overcoat and pinstriped suit would sit across from Rogan. Rogan always had pancakes; his dad preferred eggs and toast.

"You know he'd be proud of you," said McKenzie.

"Who?"

"Him," said McKenzie nodding towards the indentation. "You took a life, but you saved a couple others, and you solved the case. Your dad would be proud."

"Thanks Mac, and I'm sorry," said Rogan.

"Sorry for what?"

"Putting you in danger like that. If I wouldn't have gotten so wrapped up in the case, you wouldn't have gotten kidnapped."

"Oh stop it. I'm not that little girl with pigtails anymore, you know?"

"I know, but you're all I have left, Mac. I don't want anything to happen to you."

"Rogan, I knew a long time ago that hanging out with you would mean breaking some laws once in a while and occasionally dodging a bullet. I'm good with it. "

"Okay, but next time we need to be more careful."

"Next time?"

"Yeah, I don't think I can just chase ghosts anymore."

"Kinda figured. So what now?"

"I think I'm going to get my Private Investigator's license."

"Well then that P.I. on your business card will finally make some sense."

"Oh that one's staying. I'm thinking, Richard Rogan – P.I., P.I."

The End

About the Author:

Keith Allen lives in South Dakota with his fantastically supportive wife Becky and his best friend/dog, Callie.

Would you like to be the first to hear about New Releases from Keith Allen, including Evergreen, the sequel to Heartless?

Sign up for his New Release Mailinglist:
http://www.KeithAllenAuthor.com/mailinglist

Other ways to communicate with Keith Allen:
Website: http://www.KeithAllenAuthor.com
Twitter: http://www.twitter.com/KeithAllenBooks

www.ingramcontent.com/pod-product-compliance
Lightning Source LLC
Chambersburg PA
CBHW020055180626
46812CB00006B/2344